LIKE HELL

LIKE HELL

a novel by Ben Foster

Hope And Nonthings

Hope And Nonthings
www.hopeandnonthings.com

Printed in the United States Of America
First printing: May 2001

First edition

ISBN # 0-9707458-2-6, Library of Congress Control Number: 2001088972

Cover art: Felice Eliscu

<u>ACKNOWLEDGMENTS</u>

The author wishes to express his thanks to the people who have helped him with encouragement, suggestions, editing and support in general in writing this book: Rachel Cohn, Sara Corrigan, Steven Malk, John Pierson, Paul Thomas and Sabina Vavra. Consider yourselves acknowledged.

ASSHOLE

ONE

I stopped drinking Budweiser when I realized it was fucking up my sex life. I don't know what it was, but there was something in a 12-ounce Bud longneck that went straight to my dick and hit the Down button. I was about to turn twenty-one and I was drinking like a fool and fools and Budweiser seem to have a mutual attraction. The Kid was playing bass in the band at the time. He was still in high school but he didn't make a habit of attending classes. That put him over at my place, sitting across from me at the kitchen table, both of us in front of a six pack of Bud longnecks.

"I fucked my girlfriend in the ass last night," he'd say.

I'd start laughing hysterically.

"I got some sort of sticky gross stuff all over my dick."

"That's called shit, Kid."

"No," he'd say, screwing his face up in disgust at the thought of what I'd suggested and the fact that I'd suggested it. "It wasn't shit. I know shit when I see it."

"Did you use lube?"

"My spit."

"It was shit."

And so forth. Budweiser doesn't only ruin your sex life, it turns you into a moron.

****

Maybe 1989 was going to be a good year. I'd just moved out of an apartment I'd been sharing with a skinhead and an anarchist - that had been a real riot - and Jimmy and I were staying at Don's apartment in Wrigleyville. The band had released two records on Don's little bedroom label. The records weren't exactly burning up the charts; in fact the band was a pretty expensive hobby. Jimmy played guitar in the band and worked at a coffee shop. I sang and played second guitar and worked at a news agency delivering the *Sun-Times*. Any money above rent, food and beer went into the band fund. The always empty band fund. Most people had never heard of our band. Most of the ones who *had* heard us thought we sucked. But it was a way to kill the boredom of job after job. Have a little fun. Write some dumb tunes, get up on a stage, sweat, scream, stomp, spit, sometimes bleed and get ten, maybe twenty bucks for our efforts. We thought we had it pretty good. Subsisting on Ramen, pasta, rice and beans; occasionally splurging on a sandwich at the deli on the corner.

After four years of doing the band it was getting hard to remember why we'd started and why we kept bothering to keep it going. I mean, I knew logically why - me and Jimmy had discovered punk rock at the same time and we'd had the same epiphany that so many people before us had: "Hey, why can't *we* do this?" - but after having gone through three drummers and two bass players already; after losing so much money on tours; after using all the money we could raise to pay for recording albums that never broke even; after starting to feel like it was becoming pointless because we weren't getting any more popular; after all that, the novelty had worn off. I guess we kept doing it because hanging out in the rehearsal space working on new tunes for a record or tightening up old ones for a gig was still fun. Just playing never got old, but most of what went on outside of that practice room sure did. Twenty-one meant I was an adult. All the things besides the music that had attracted me to punk in the first place - the strong sense of individuality that I thought all real punks had, the refusal to buy into the accepted truths of mainstream society, the idea that you didn't have to give in and be like everyone else to get through life - I still felt all that was true, but I had to learn the downside of it the hard way. And the downside was moving around from apartment to apartment, working shitty jobs for low pay and having everybody in your life who wasn't a punk look down on you.

There was only one bedroom in the apartment, which was Don's. Me and Jimmy got the floor of the living room. At least it was carpeted. I slept on three couch cushions I'd scavenged from an old hide-a-bed. Jimmy just slept on the floor with a sleeping bag and a ratty old blanket. He was hardly ever home so I usually got the whole floor to myself.

Don owned the record label but me and Jimmy did most of the work. For free, of course; there was no money in punk. Don was a free-lance writer and an early riser. If I wasn't getting woken up at seven a.m. by the construction crew across the courtyard with their jackhammers and bulldozers, it was Don clanking away on the goddamned computer keyboard. I got in from work at around five a.m., and I usually drank a six-pack of Bud before hitting the sack, so seven was a little early for me. Sometimes I managed to fall back asleep, but more often than not I just laid there on the floor, grinding my teeth, feeling the rage build up. If I didn't drink Budweiser before going to bed, I'm sure I would've slept right through all that.

****

The Kid came over with some pot one morning. He didn't know how to roll a joint.

"It's been a while," I said. "But I'll give it a shot."

I rolled a fat joint and lit it for him.

"You don't want any?"

"No. Yeah. What the fuck."

I hadn't smoked weed in years, since before I'd been thrown into rehab. It tasted awful. I was completely stoned before we'd even finished the joint. The Kid asked me something. A few minutes later, I turned my head.

"Wha-a-a-t?"

He just broke up.

"You're stoned!"

"Yeah, I guess so..."

I turned on the television. Bert and Ernie.

"Fuck those guys," I said. "They're not supporting the scene." Budweiser made my dick limp. Pot obliterated my sense of wit.

"They sold out!" The Kid was *cackling*. "Fuckin' TV stars! I'm writing a letter to *Punk Bible*." That was the New York fanzine that was the watchdog of the punk rock scene for the entire world. And I was one of the smart-ass columnists, still young enough to be pedantic and outrageously naive but cynical and incredulous enough about the politically correct behavior of punks - even as my own attitudes and behavior often contradicted my self-righteous diatribes - to keep the hate mail pouring in.

"Yeah!" yelled The Kid. "Sell-out motherfuckers! There's your next column!"

The Kid wasn't exactly batting a thousand in the humor department either but I laughed anyway, knowing I was an idiot for laughing and not caring.

We listened to some records and we were so stoned we thought they were all good.

****

That night, around six, The Kid came by with his girlfriend.

"You wanna get high?" he asked.

"I should wait for Sylvia."

The Kid's girlfriend gave him a look. That cunt look. That "do something about this" look.

"When's she getting here?" he asked, embarrassed.

"Fuck it. Where's the papers?"

"I lost 'em."

"Idiot."

I went into the kitchen and searched around in the fridge until I found a can of Bud in the crisper. I popped it and drank it down, then caved in the middle about a quarter of the way with my thumbs. We all searched around for a pin or a tack or a needle. Nobody could find one so I poked a few holes in the middle of the can with a pen, which resulted in much larger holes than we needed. The Kid placed some weed on top of the holes, put his mouth to the opening of the can and lit the makeshift pipe.

By the time Sylvia showed up the pot was gone and we were stoned. She was pissed that we'd gotten high without her.

"You don't even smoke pot," I reminded her.

"Neither do you."

I was getting all wiggy like I do when I get high. I wanna move my leg to the left a little, but will it look weird? It would certainly be more comfortable. But will it look suspicious, like I'm shifting around nervously? What's everybody gonna think if I move my leg? And why am I even thinking like this? Jesus Christ, I'm a fucking mess! I gotta get a drink of water. Stand up, come on, stand up. Walk to the kitchen, turn on the water, fill the glass. The water's piss warm. Dump it in the sink. Shit, I'm being rude. Poke my head around the corner.

"Anybody want water?"

Nobody wants water, but they're looking at me all strange. I *am* all strange. Fill the glass again, go back and sit down on the floor, drink the water down. I'm still thirsty but I'm not going through that bullshit again. I'll be thirsty.

The Kid and his girlfriend left after a while and Sylvia started fooling around with my crotch.

"You're cute when you're high."

"I'm paranoid when I'm high."

She was determined to make me horny, working on my dick through my jeans. The last thing I wanted to do was fuck.

"Not now, pussycat."

"Now."

Pot always brought out the Catholic guilt in me. It also made me too lazy to argue. I laid down on the floor and she unbuttoned my jeans and pulled them down to my knees. My dick was all shriveled up. She put it in her mouth and started sucking it slowly. After a few weeks, it got semi-hard. She took her clothes off, really fast and businesslike. She never liked wasting time undressing. She got on her back and I kneeled in front of her. She grabbed my dick and guided it towards her pussy. Still wet from her mouth, it slid in easily. I fucked her mechanically, like one of those plastic cocktail birds that bobs its head to drink from your glass. I could feel her pubic hair rubbing against mine like a Brillo pad. I came inside her as soon as I could, pulled out and started dressing. She was laying on the floor naked, laughing like crazy.

"That was weird," she finally said.

I stumbled over my pants leg and landed on my shoulder. After swearing loudly for a few seconds, I said, "Yeah. I'm weird."

****

Weird. Crazy. Freak. Punk motherfucker. Whether they were unspoken by family members and co-workers or shouted out passing car windows by frat boys and cheerleaders, these were the words that defined us in the eyes of others. And we accepted them with a defiant pride because at least it made us different from them. If you saw a guy with spiked hair and a Ramones t-shirt walking down Clark Street carrying a duffel bag, he was a kindred spirit; an out of town punk who'd probably end up spending a week at your apartment. You shared your food and your floor space and if you were ever in his town, you knew he'd do the same for you. The haircuts, t-shirts, leather jackets, patches, badges, tattoos and piercings were all signs for other punks to approach you as a friend. There were always phonies and creeps and assholes around, but more often than not you made friends with complete strangers in minutes; at a show, a bar, a coffee shop, a diner, a bus stop. It didn't matter if they liked bands you hated or if they were anarchists or communists and you were apolitical; in fact, arguing about that stuff was part of the fun. By and large, we stuck together - never in groups or for long periods of time - but long enough to learn each other's made-up punk names and whether we published a fanzine or played in a band or promoted shows or made fliers, and almost everybody did something like that. I'd gone through phases of being a punk: a straight edge phase, a political phase, a fuck-the-world phase, but I'd finally decided that the punks were never going to change the world; and at a couple of weeks shy of twenty-one, I was just a punk rocker playing in a band and that's all I needed to be. I'd been involved with political movements and punk collectives but they always fell apart. Punks just didn't work well together; too many chiefs and only a handful of Indians. I'd been disappointed at first, but now I was grateful that I'd finally stopped deluding myself about what punk meant. Punks didn't question the meaning of life; the question was "What is punk?" It would be argued forever but I already figured I knew the answer. Punk was playing, promoting or writing about loud, fast, simple music; and it was an inherent inability to fit in with society. And nobody could tell me different. Even within the band we had our differences: for Jimmy it was simply another form of music; for The Kid it was fashion and action; for Howie it was a part-time thing, a brief phase before he grew up and moved on to the real world, which was going to happen as soon as he got a real job to start paying for college in the Fall. But for me it was about never having fit in wherever I'd been for as long as I'd been alive and learning to wear that badge of rejection with pride. I'd passed the point of sour grapes years before and actually learned to enjoy being an outcast. I seldom thought about the future, but when I did it was always in terms of what I could never do and never be, and knowing all those things I could never do or be comforted me, at least when I was among my own kind. You always feel better when you know where you stand in the world. I was a punk, and I'd always be one because I didn't have any choice in the matter.

TWO

We borrowed a van from an anarchist collective that only charged twenty bucks for in-state gigs and thirty for anything out of state; there were about ten local punk bands that used it regularly. Howie was playing his last gig with us in St. Louis.

We already had a new drummer lined up, an impossibly tall guy named Vic. He must've been at least six foot six and he looked even taller 'cause he was so skinny. He kept his head shaved but he didn't hang out with the skinheads. He was always alone and people knew better than to fuck with him; he didn't need a gang backing him up. He'd been coming to our shows for the past few years, always up in front stage-diving and slam-dancing. Vic had gone to the same high school as me and Jimmy for his first year and we'd known him by sight but then he'd disappeared - nobody knew where he'd gone. I'd disappeared too, into rehab for a year, but I'd kept in touch with Jimmy. Vic had taken a different path. When we ran into him at a show a year after we'd dropped out, he told us he'd gone up to Canada and played junior hockey in the OHL for a while as a defenseman; his folks were filthy rich and could afford to send him off to pursue a career in beating the shit out of other people while wearing ice skates. He'd done okay at first, but after a couple of years he'd been banned from the league for life for cross-checking a ref in the face during a bench-clearing brawl. He'd told me he probably could've gotten a gig in the Colonial League where they loved goons, or the East Coast League - known as the Cocktail League by most players - where all you had to do was show up and drag yourself over to the bench, but he'd never scored a goal and he was a slow, clumsy skater; all he ever really did was fight, and he loved playing music so much he was afraid he'd permanently fuck up his hands during a brawl and never be able to hold a drum stick again. Besides all that, the NHL scouts were wary of him early on because he always acted so goofy on the ice. He used to take bows after winning fights and sometimes he'd kick guys with his skates once he'd beaten them down. He'd even pulled a Hanson Brothers move a couple of times, going after fans up in the stands. But what really sealed his fate was when he showed up at a playoff game sporting a mohawk; that one silly little incident pretty much blew his already slim chances of ever making it to the NHL. He wore a bridge to take the place of his four missing front teeth and he had a scar going from his upper lip to just past his left nostril, the result of a puck to the mouth courtesy of a misplaced slapshot by a teammate. Other than that, the only remnants of his short-lived career in hockey were a bent nose and a huge tattoo of a skeleton holding a hockey stick like a baseball bat that covered his right arm from shoulder to elbow. Howie was a good guy but he wanted to go back to school. Vic had no such aspirations; he would fit in perfectly. He came with us to the gig.

As usual, a gang of skinheads showed up and started shoving people around. Well, the smallest one would shove people around. If anybody shoved back, the big skins would jump in and beat the shit out of the shovee for being dumb enough to stand up for himself. I finally stopped the band in the middle of a song and addressed the little skin.

"Yo, what the fuck are you doing?"

"What? Fuck you!"

"No, fuck *you*." The other skins gathered around him. We were outnumbered, unless you counted the crowd, and it was never safe to count on the crowd. But I was oblivious to the danger, with a bellyful of Bud and a head full of righteousness.

"Do you sniff your mother's panties?" I yelled.

"What the fuck did you say? Say it again!"

"Get your nose out of your mother's underwear drawer and listen. I'm saying I think you're a pervert. You're probably queer. You've been getting so close to all the boys in the crowd that you're obviously getting some sort of homoerotic gratification out of it." I glanced down at his crotch. "Are those cum stains on your jeans?"

He looked down instinctively, which pissed him off even more. Miraculously, before the skins could kick my head in, the crowd surrounded them. A huge fight broke out; I guess it was more of a minor riot. We grabbed our gear and bailed. By the time we'd loaded the gear, the crowd had dispersed and the skins were nowhere to be found. I walked back to the club by myself, like an idiot, and managed to get twenty bucks out of the promoter; he was happy just to pay me off and get me out of there.

I walked out the back door and headed for the van. The next thing I remember was waking up in the County Hospital in St. Louis with a hell of a headache. Jimmy was standing next to the bed.

"They were waiting for you. I'm sorry. I should've gone with you."

"Why, so you could get half-killed, too? What happened?"

"The little guy hit you on the back of the head with a beer bottle."

"Fuckin' St. Louis. When's the last time anything good ever happened in this fuckin' town?"

"They ran like hell as soon as you hit the ground," he continued, oblivious to my mini-editorial on the Gateway to the West. "I think they thought they'd killed you. You got eight stitches and a mild concussion. Not that bad, really. They're gonna let you go tonight. Man, you were bleeding like crazy."

"What kind of bottle was it?"

"What?"

"What kind of beer?"

"I think it was Budweiser."

Naturally.

****

My twenty-first birthday came and went and nobody remembered except Sylvia. Birthdays were important to her.

Anniversaries too. It was easy to remember her birthday - it was on Halloween. But I always fucked up the anniversary even though it was only two weeks after her birthday. And she always got pissed off and she always forgave me. But the girl never forgot.

I didn't know what I was doing. Heady, maybe, with the rush of having a couple of thousand people in the world who gave a fuck about my band. Playing the rock star trip, even though we could barely draw a hundred people to a gig. Trying to fuck as many girls as possible, knowing I was a shit for cheating on Sylvia. I knew the gig wouldn't last forever. If some girl wanted to fuck me because I played in a band she liked, who was I to turn her down? Loyalty to Sylvia? She'd have plenty of time for me to be loyal when the band ended and nobody gave a shit about us anymore. Aside from standing on a stage playing idiotic songs and baiting the crowd, I really didn't have a whole hell of a lot else going for me. I was average looking at best - brown hair when I wasn't dyeing it, brown eyes, ears a little too long and lips a little too thin for my face, but average height and weight for my age. Nothing about me would have set me apart from a million other guys. But being in a band gets you laid. And I didn't want to miss the opportunity because I knew it wouldn't be there very long. I knew what I was. Most of the time, I didn't care.

<u>THREE</u>

I drove out to Sylvia's house in the suburbs 'cause she liked me to spend time with her folks. I don't know why. They sure as hell didn't like me.

I sat there on the couch with her stepfather sitting across from me, looking like he'd just wiped me off the bottom of his shoe. Sylvia always left me alone with him while she chattered away with her mother in the kitchen.

"Whattya call that haircut again?"

"It's a mohawk. I've told you that a hundred times."

"It's kinda stupid, don't you think?"

"Yes, Dwayne, I think it's stupid. Why else would I cut it this way? I enjoy looking stupid. Makes it easier to get people to throw quarters in my cup at the El stops."

He laughed. "Wanna beer?"

"Yeah." He only drank Old Style. He went into the kitchen and got two cans.

"So, ya ever gonna get a job?"

It was the same old shit I had to listen to every time I made the mistake of going over there. The guy didn't really care; he was just doing Sylvia's mom's dirty work. She never said a word to me about work. Her eyes did all her talking. And her dopey mouthpiece of a husband. I popped the beer and swallowed half of it before I answered.

"I have a job. At the agency."

"Oh yeah," he said, like he hadn't remembered. "But Irene says you're quitting to go run around the country."

"I'm going on tour with the band. We have two albums out, y'know?"

"Oh yeah. What's the name of that band again?"

"Pagan Icons."

"Ho ho!" I mean, he actually said, "Ho-ho." Why hadn't I made up an excuse, any excuse, for not coming?

"So what does that pay?"

I belched, long and loud. "I reap the rewards of a life fully lived." That threw him off - he was genuinely dense.

"Listen," he said, leaning forward in his La-Z-Boy, all pissed off now, like an orangutan after somebody swiped his bananas, "I work hard for a living. If I want a taco, or a burrito, or a set of snow tires, I can just go buy 'em. You can't. You have to borrow money from Sylvia. A *girl!*" He sat back, triumphant and practically glowing over the most scathing verbal attack he'd ever delivered.

"Dude, I don't need any snow tires. What are you talking about?"

"I'm talking about why don't you get a real job and keep it for more than two months? I'm talking about why don't you get your shit together?"

"Dwayne, you're not in the Army anymore."

"And you're not a teenager anymore, smart-ass. You're walking around with that stupid blue mohawk looking like a goddamned fool. You know people are laughing at you behind your back?"

"Gimme some names and I'll have them killed."

"Yeah you're real funny, buddy..."

"Listen, man. I heard this fuckin' lecture from teachers and shrinks and cops all through high school and I heard it from my parents a thousand times, and if you really wanna bore me, keep on with it, but if you think I'm gonna take you seriously, you're nuts."

"Look, look, look," he said. "I don't mean anything. I'm just trying to help you." He was used to backpedalling, being with Sylvia's mom. "Y'know, I can get you a good job on the loading dock at McNeeley. Full benefits after six months."

"Thanks, Dwayne," I said. "But I'd rather fuck around with my stupid band if you don't mind too much."

Dwayne was completely pussywhipped, so when Sylvia's mother came in and said she was going out to find some new shrubs or something for the front yard, he put his ass in gear and got his hat and coat.

****

I would never let Dwayne know, but I was pissed off, the way I always got when I found myself thinking about my future. I knew the guy was a buffoon, but who the hell was I? I didn't have any health insurance. I didn't have any car insurance. I didn't own any furniture. I slept on some guy's floor, on three couch cushions, for chrissakes. I had no skills, no schooling, and no talent. It wasn't like my band was going anywhere. We wanted to be like the Ramones but we just weren't good enough. I wrote all the songs - if you could call them that. Short, fast, loud bursts of noise with a tiny germ of a tune somewhere in the background if you listened closely enough. The words were more important than the music because words were all I really had. Our biggest asset, the only thing that really set us apart from a thousand other bands, was our unfailing ability to get people worked up; pounding bolts in the heads of their sacred cows: anarchism, socialism, communism, apathy, love, hate, eating meat, not eating meat, being a drunk, being straight edge, being a punk, being a skinhead; if people took it seriously, I attacked it. When everybody was anti-Reagan I wrote "Right Wing Is Right." When everybody was talking about religion being the opium of the masses, I wrote "Jesus Was A Punk Rocker." And when that stuff got the skinheads cheering for us, I wrote "Bald And Dickless." I thought cops were easy to piss off until I played my first punk gig. I hated Reagan, I was an atheist and I had a couple of skinhead friends but that wasn't the point; the idea was to drive people to the point of wanting to kill you without actually pushing them over the edge so that you ended up in a hospital bed, even though that sometimes happened. It was just a dumb little game, but we were good at it. It wasn't so much that the average punk didn't have a sense of humor; they had no perspective. Some of the punks, the ones I thought were the real punks, understood it. They got it. They realized it was all an enormous joke and that we were too, but that we knew it. But so many of them couldn't see beyond the convenient black and white world they'd set up for themselves, couldn't see they were really just like their parents. Twenty years from now they'd be showing their kids photos from the old days. "This was back in my wild days, son, when I was a punk rocker. Then I wised up and got a job with IBM." But the fucked up part about it was that I knew I wasn't really any different. Only I wasn't going to be working for IBM. I'd be in some warehouse or a factory, delivering pizzas or trimming bushes and laying sod. Sitting around all bitter and mean, wishing I was back in the good old days. Well, if you know the good old days are going to end, you might as well enjoy 'em while they're here.

And I tried to just enjoy it, but it was getting harder not to worry. I was spending too much time freaking out about my future and I knew it was stupid, 'cause where does it end? When you're dead, that's when, so what was the point? And who the fuck was Dwayne to say anything to me anyway? Jesus Christ, I had enough problems without that half-bald, bearded motherfucker giving me shit. I mean, the guy worked in a warehouse. I'm supposed to be impressed?

****

Sylvia made some mac and cheese for lunch and I grabbed a couple of Dwayne's beers. We sat around watching TV for a few minutes, me trying to look at her without her noticing I was looking at her 'cause it always made her uncomfortable. She was pretty, but not in any conventional way and she dragged her hang-ups about her appearance around with her like a heavy suitcase. She had a sharp, cruel face but there was a joy and a childlike curiosity in her eyes, except when she was pissed. Half German and half Czech, her pale skin appeared to be frigid and unforgiving but was surprisingly warm; the gypsy in her had won that battle. The volatile combination of that cold/passionate blood running through her veins had made her a dangerous contradiction. She could be sweet and compassionate but would quickly turn cold and nasty at the slightest offense. Her short, spiked, black hair was the exclamation point on the top of a four foot ten stick of dynamite. She even *fucked* mean like a chronically horny rabid dog. And she felt no guilt. Never felt bad about acting like a whore with me. She saw it as her right. She hated feminists, but she was the truest feminist I ever met. She'd fuck like an animal for half an hour, then turn around and get dressed for work. Smiling face, friendly to the customers, always on time, perfect employee. Drunk out of her mind at four a.m. giving me head in the church parking lot, then sitting in the pew like an angel at nine. She knew she led a double life and she was proud of it. And as much as I tried to convince myself that I'd never live like that, that it was a cop-out, I envied her and the ease with which she shifted roles.

She caught me looking at her and instead of getting pissed and asking me if I had a staring problem like she usually did, she unbuttoned my jeans and stood up, holding onto my dick, and led me down the hall. When she tried to take a left into her room, I gave her a little nudge towards her mother's bedroom. We went over to the exercise bike in the corner and I pulled her pants down and bent her over the handlebars.

"Nice ass."

"It's flabby."

"No, it isn't," I lied.

I slapped it a few times.

"Fuck me," she said.

We fucked hard and fast and when we'd both gotten off she turned around and kissed me. We made out for a few minutes, just standing there all naked and sticky.

FOUR

I drove up to Round Lake Beach - a real dump of a town - with Jimmy and Vic to look at a van for the tour. My old man had lost his job and my folks had moved up there a couple of years earlier 'cause it was cheap. Depressing, but cheap. The old man had seen some vans for sale in the paper up there and told me we could probably get a good deal. Maybe it was just an excuse for me to visit - my brother and I didn't see my folks too often and I think they were lonely. We had lunch at their place and then went and bought a big red Ford beast with the four hundred bucks Don had loaned us. By the time we got back to my folks' house the van was already billowing out smoke like crazy - there was an oil leak. My folks just laughed at me. Typical. They thought it was hilarious. Maybe that's what happens when you have kids; you spend years trying to mold them and shape them and they keep squirming away and they keep on fucking up, and then when they hit eighteen and you get them out of the house after having nearly given yourself a stroke and three heart attacks trying to keep 'em out of jail and in school, then you can finally relax; sit back and laugh when they act like jackasses. They deserved it. After all they'd put up with from me as a teenager - the drugs, the courts, the shrinks, the rehab center - I guess they'd earned the right to smirk.

Me and Vic drove the van back and Jimmy followed us in my car. I'd made sure that Jimmy had the right change for the tolls but when we went through the Deerfield plaza, we heard him stuck at the gate behind us, yelling my name: "Joe! *Jo-o-o-oe!*" I thought it was funny as hell. I kept driving; if he was dumb enough to follow us into the exact change lane without the exact change, then let him suffer the terrible consequences.

I used the van for my Sunday route a few times. Everybody in the warehouse got all pissed off when I'd back it into the loading dock, 'cause it farted out so much horrible oily smoke, but it was a hell of a lot easier using the van for my route than my car, and it wasn't like the mooks at the agency were my friends. Fuck 'em.

The Kid was coming with me on my route a lot - I gave him twenty-five bucks a week to help me out on Sundays - and I liked to send him to the back of the van for papers and then start swerving around on the road to sort of play human pinball with him. The Kid didn't appreciate my sense of humor but I guess he didn't have anything better to do at four a.m. on Sunday mornings. His real name was Bill but everybody called him "Kid" - even his folks - because he was so small. He was short, skinny and weird looking, with albino-white hair, a lazy eye and a bunch of tattoos of logos of old punk rock bands covering his arms. I guess he liked me enough to put up with my shit but I got more than a couple of Sunday papers whipped at my head when I took things too far. Which I usually did.

Vic was working out okay on drums. He wasn't the greatest drummer but he practiced on his own a lot and he was getting better. We were all pretty lousy musicians anyway. We hadn't played a show with him yet 'cause we'd been busy working on a new EP called *Fistfucker*. Vic was an alcoholic-in-training, even more than me, but I didn't really spend much time with him. He hung out at bars most of the time, which wasn't really my thing. We ended up playing our first gig with him on drums down in Cicero at a bar run by an old musician from some briefly famous pop band from the '60s who'd decided to allow some punks to promote a few all-ages shows every month.

Right before the set, I pulled on a pair of yellow leotards that Jimmy and I had found at a shop out in the suburbs - I had a hell of a time making the saleswoman think me and Jimmy were a couple of queers while I tried on various leotards - and I downed four or five beers, and Vic and The Kid had a few as well. I had to be on my toes 'cause I wasn't just singing, I was playing guitar as well, and I'm no musician; I have to pay attention to what I'm doing. But I knew my limits. The Kid never did. He'd only been in the band for a few months and I'd tried to talk to him a few times about cutting down on his drinking before a gig but it was hard to make an effective argument when I had a beer in my hand. He was worse than usual tonight. He was drunk and trying to play bass and sing backing vocals, but he was fucking everything up. And worse, between every other song, he would lean over to the mic and ask an audience member to go get him another beer. And since he was fucking up so much it was fucking Vic up. Vic had drank a lot by then but he seemed to be able to handle it well - in fact it didn't seem to have much effect on him at all. It was obvious that he was fumbling mostly because The Kid was all over the place on the bass.

After the show, I found The Kid at the bar and told him that I wasn't fucking around anymore.

"From now on," I said, "no more than two beers before we play. Band Rule Number 28." And he said okay, but he was so hammered I didn't know if he'd remember it tomorrow. And then I noticed that the little devil was surrounded by, like, five girls. Sylvia had to work that night which meant I was all alone and feeling a little horny, so I started getting friendly with one of the girls, a skinny little punk named Patty. She was wearing black leather pants and a red t-shirt with the sleeves cut off to show off the Germs tattoo on her shoulder and she had that dyed blonde hair that's almost white, and her eyebrows were dark brown, which I found really hot - maybe because her hair was so obviously dyed and she either didn't realize it or didn't give a fuck.

I knew I shouldn't be fucking around on Sylvia but I couldn't seem to help it. Patty was right in front of me. Sylvia wasn't. Somehow, in my alcohol-soaked brain, it all made sense. If the guilt really starts bugging you, just have another beer...

I took Patty out back to the van. And next thing, she's on her hands and knees and I'm fucking the shit out of her and the van's bucking around like crazy. We take a little break and we're just sitting there, sweating and breathing all heavy, when the back door of the van swings open and there's Jimmy about to heave his Marshall inside, and he's looking at me with my jeans at my ankles and Patty with her tail up in the air. Jimmy's face goes bright red and he shuts the door and I start fucking Patty again, and we get off. And there's no Kleenex in the van, so I find an oily rag and wipe the cum off my dick and off her ass. And we get dressed and go next door to the coffee shop.

The Kid has already left with his brother and Jimmy and Vic come in and tell me the van's loaded up. So I say, okay, let's go, and Jimmy, you gotta drive 'cause I'm drunk; the last thing we need right before the tour is a DWI.

"Joe, I'm not gonna drive that thing," says Jimmy.

"Well," says I, "you gotta. I'm fuckin' blasted."

But Jimmy is not getting behind the wheel. And Vic's ingested so much Budweiser he's not even worth considering. So we sit around with Patty and a few of her friends, and I'm pissed 'cause I don't wanna be sitting here downing cup after cup of black coffee, and Vic's pissed 'cause there's a party at a motel up on Elston Avenue and he's got a shot at getting laid, and Jimmy's just sitting there, refusing to drive.

So we just shoot the shit with the girls for a while, and I notice that Patty's got a pretty ugly sore on the corner of her mouth. I hadn't noticed it 'cause we hadn't kissed. I'm thinking, fuck, maybe the girl gave me herpes or some fucking thing. I mean, I don't know the difference between mouth herpes and genital herpes. And it would make perfect sense if I were to get some wicked Catholic payback for not kissing her before I fucked her.

Finally I get tired of sitting around, and everybody piles in the van, Jimmy riding shotgun, and we take off, and I'm steamed 'cause if I get pulled over I'm losing my license. We get off the highway, dump Vic and the girls at the motel and head for home. By the time we're almost back to the apartment, I gotta take a leak bad, too bad to wait another six blocks, so I pull over, get out and piss up against the south wall of Wrigley Field. I piss so much that when I'm done I don't even feel drunk anymore.

When we get home, I decide I'm not so mad at Jimmy anymore. But I still owe him one.

FIVE

I couldn't stay pissed at Jimmy for very long. He was my oldest friend. He hardly ever complained, not like the other band members.

Jimmy came from a poor family. He'd been working since he was twelve - he got me my first job washing dishes when I was thirteen - and he never had much money but he always managed to dress sharp and he always had a perfectly shaped flat-top. I don't know if he was buddies with the barber and the people at the clothes shops or what, but the guy always looked impeccable.

He was a year older than me, and that seems like a big deal when you're a kid, but we were best friends. We'd grown up together just a block away from each other; played Little League ball on the same team; took up smoking together at the age of eleven; built forts and rope swings by the creek in the fields behind our neighborhood, and blazed trails through those fields for our little RM-80's; smoked our first joint together. Hell, our first girlfriends were sisters.

I guess we knew each other pretty well 'cause he knew enough to let me go on with my crazy schemes, always doing everything the hard way, and I knew enough to know when to push him and when to lay off. He didn't expect much out of the band, so whenever he got anything he was happy. Just happy to be in a band, playing guitar. It was an odd situation 'cause Jimmy didn't drink too much; he'd straightened up in high school and he had his shit together a lot more than I did, but I was running the show. The lush. The hothead. The overgrown juvenile delinquent. But we worked well together. Maybe he saw a method to my madness. Most of the time, I sure didn't. I knew this: it wouldn't last long. I wasn't gonna end up like those other old-time punk bands, a golden oldies act. And that was assuming we ever got the chance, which was a long shot at best. Our mission was to have some fun, piss a lot of people off and then... well, I guess play for a couple more years, watch the band die out and start working towards a pension plan at a warehouse or a factory. It would be nice, though, if we ever managed to get out of debt and sell more than a couple thousand records...

****

The van shit the bed. It had lasted for three weeks. I called the junkyard that advertises on TV and they gave me fifty bucks for it before towing it away.

"So what are we gonna do?" asked Jimmy.

"I don't know. I already told 'em at the agency that I'm quitting. And I'm sick of sitting around here."

"Can we take your car?"

"Where are we gonna put all our gear?"

"I dunno, maybe we could get a U-Haul trailer and hook it up to the bumper."

It seemed like a halfway decent idea. We'd already spent a lot of money on long distance to book the tour, so we might as well go do it. My '73 Nova was covered with rust and Bondo spots but it ran well.

It turned out that it would cost too much to put a hitch on the Nova, but we were able to borrow one of those carrier things that you clamp to the top of your car from The Duke. The Duke was the Head Drunk of the ShitHole, always getting young punk girls into bed just by having an English accent and a cocky attitude; never mind the horrifying teeth and the rotten body stench - there were plenty of chicks who thought a real Brit was a real punk. I promised The Duke that in return we'd mention him in a song for whatever we recorded next and it was a done deal. We could throw our clothes, t-shirt screen and a couple of boxes of records in the carrier, lay out our sleeping bags on the seats, and put our guitars, a snare and a bass drum pedal in the trunk, and we'd just borrow gear from opening bands on the road. We decided that was the only way to go, and we wanted to go.

Three days before we were leaving, we had sort of a going away party at the ShitHole, a punk house in a loft on the fourth floor of an abandoned building in Irving Park. When we walked in there was already a keg there and Sylvia was there too, drunk on vodka.

We got into it, and the long and the short of it was that she was convinced I was fucking around on her. And why not?

Of course, I did the stupid thing. I told her the truth. Most of it, anyway. I walked her down to the corner, and we sat down on a stoop in front of a liquor store and I told her. And she started screaming at me. And some joker from the party walked by and laughed at me. Perfect.

"You fucking cocksucker," she screamed. "You made me look like a fool!"

"You don't look like a fool, pussycat."

She whacked me on the arm real good for that one.

"Listen, goddamnit," I said, asserting myself with drunken pride, "I don't need this shit right now. I'm about to go out on the road. I told you the truth, and I'm sorry, and it's over. What the fuck do you want?"

This, of course, brought on a barrage of mostly incoherent screaming and yelling.

We ended up back at the party, where Sylvia promptly passed out on a couch. The band played and I got hammered. Sylvia woke up at one point, just long enough to lob a beer bottle in my direction and puke all over the floor before she passed out again.

****

You bet your *ass* I was glad to get on the road. And not a single promoter from Chicago to Seattle would book us, so we had to drive all the way to Olympia, Washington to start the tour. That's what happens when you don't have a booking agent but you insist on touring anyway, booking the shows yourself. You get what you pay for. Me and Jimmy scraped up enough money to pay for gas to get us out to the coast and Vic stole some fruit, peanut butter and bread from the supermarket where he worked, loading in boxes of food and mopping floors. That would at least get us out to Olympia. We'd have to drive straight through taking shifts; there wasn't any money for motels.

We were at a gas station in the middle of Wyoming when an old guy with Arizona plates on his Cadillac came over to us.

"You from Chicago?" Illinois plates, city sticker, I wonder what gave us away.

"Yeah."

"Me too," he said, smiling. "I used to live over by Irving and Narraganset."

"I'm at Irving and Cicero, Six Corners," said The Kid.

"Addison and Halsted," I said.

"Oh, over by the ball park."

"Yeah, and I got the parking tickets to prove it."

The Kid and the old guy talked for a while about the guy's old neighborhood, then the geezer wished us luck and bailed out. We sat on the hood of the Nova eating peanut butter on white bread. Spreading the peanut butter with a screwdriver, 'cause we didn't have a knife.

****

By the time we got into Olympia, there was a huge bubble on the driver's side front tire. We pulled over to fill up at the first gas station we saw in town. I got out and the tire started to go flat right in front of me. Me and Jimmy put the spare on and we drove to the promoter's apartment. She ordered a pizza for us - half pepperoni for Vic - and after we ate, we headed to the club. We hadn't slept in two days, but we loaded our gear onto the stage and hung around in the back of the room waiting to play. Tired, bored and none of us in any mood to listen to three shitty local bands playing way too long. Vic letting the foulest of farts rip every thirty seconds or so courtesy of the pepperoni we were always begging him not to eat. Get used to it, 'cause there's six more weeks of it to go.

In the middle of our set, some drunk jock shoved his way up to the front of the stage and, using the heel of his hand, smashed the mic right into my face. The curse of the singer/guitarist, always defenseless.

I felt liquid all over my face and figured I was bleeding, so I pulled off my guitar, tossed it behind me and went after the prick with the mic stand. He saw me coming and ran out of the club. He probably would've beaten the shit out of me but when you get rushed on stage all you care about is getting in a few shots and fuck the consequences. I wiped my nose with the back of my hand before I put my guitar back on and saw it wasn't blood on my face - it was just sweat and snot from where he'd caught me in the nose.

We made two hundred bucks, which was way better than we expected. Seemed like a good omen. I didn't get laid after the show - I was trying to reform for Sylvia's sake - but I did get drunk, so it was a good night.

SIX

We drove down to the Bay Area the next day. I'd booked a gig at The Warehouse in Oakland and Jimmy had booked us at a club in San Francisco, and between them, we had a gig up in Petaluma.

Colleen put us up at her place in El Sobrante for three days. I stayed drunk on King Cobra - the ghetto version of Bud - the whole time. The day after the Warehouse gig we went back down to Oakland and recorded a couple of songs on an sixteen-track recorder in a makeshift studio in a storefront for a compilation record. We had four hours to record and mix two songs, which wouldn't have been a problem except that we only had one new song written.

"Gimme a minute," I said. I grabbed a cold forty of King Cobra and sat down outside on the sidewalk with my notepad. Within a few minutes I had the lyrics for a song called "Suck My Pussy." I went back inside and explained the song structure to the guys.

"See, at the beginning it's just me shouting the words and then when I say "Fuck you!," that's the beginning of the chorus and you guys all come in - drums and guitars - on the word 'you'."

"Where?" asked The Kid.

"I said, on 'you'."

"No, I mean where on the guitar?"

"Where on the guitar? Are you kidding? Same place as always - fifth fret, E-string. Then it's just three chords for the chorus." I showed them on my guitar and Jimmy and The Kid followed along.

"Then after two runs on the chorus we do the same thing as the beginning - no guitars - only this time Vic's backing me up with a straight up four-four beat with just the kick and snare, and the guitars come in on the same place as the first time to start the chorus, but this time the chorus goes four times and then ends on "Fuck you!" on the beginning note."

"Can we run through it?" asked Vic.

"Well, I suppose if we have to..."

We ran through it three or four times - I kept having to tell Vic to speed it up - and then recorded it in one take. I wanted to sing first and then overdub my guitar track but we were running short on time; we still had to mix. But I was pretty happy with the lyrics:

I was minding my own business last night at a party at The Duke's
When a bunch of frat boys showed up calling us a bunch of pukes
The biggest one got in my face and said "You look so fuckin' gay"
So I told that prick to suck my cunt and I'd shoot it all over his ugly face

Fuck you!
Suck my pussy if you know how to
Fuck you!
And if I'm on the rag you'll suck that too

He told me I should step outside, I said "Why do you wanna dance?"
He answered, "No, you fucking queer, I'm gonna kick your ass!"
The cops showed up, saw us and them and dragged all the punks away
But just before the cuffs went on I had another chance to say

Fuck you!
Suck my pussy if you know how to
Fuck you!
And if I'm on the rag you'll suck that too
Fuck you!
Suck my clit and suck my nipples too

Fuck you!
I'd rather be a fag than be like you
Fuck you!

The guys overdubbed a gang vocal for every "Fuck you!" For a spur of the moment, minute-long tune it turned out pretty good. In fact, it was better than anything else we'd recorded before.

****

Colleen brought us to a K-Mart so we could buy white Hanes t-shirts and she let us spend the rest of the night stinking up her apartment, printing Pagan Icons t-shirts with our makeshift screen. All she wanted was for us to buy a couple rolls of toilet paper. And I think we forgot to do that...

A couple more tires went flat and we had to spend a few hundred bucks to get the car fixed so it, uhh... so it would stop making all our tires flat. Hell, we weren't mechanics, we were... well, I guess we weren't musicians either. I really don't know what we were.

****

The Hippie showed up at the Petaluma gig. We'd met him the year before in San Francisco on our second tour and quickly realized he was nuts. He wasn't *dangerous* nuts, just harmlessly crazy. His insanity was limited to narcissism countered by long periods of depression filled with self-loathing. He had the mind of a sociopath but he generally kept his warped brain in check; he was active in local grassroots political and social movements and his criminal activity was limited to medium-scale pot-dealing. He was one of those old guys who hangs around the punk scene for reasons that only they know - there was a guy like that back home, and in most of the cities we'd played. They were always a little out of place but they were invaluable when underage punks needed somebody to buy them beer. The only problem was, you always had to sit around and pretend like you were interested in their musings and lectures if you wanted something out of them and they were invariably boring as hell. The Hippie was no exception.

He owned a label called Stinkbomb Records. He had two partners, but rumor was that they were bailing out at the end of the year. Whether it was because they couldn't stand being around a fat, smelly, bearded freak or because he revelled in playing mind games, constantly pitting them against each other - even pitting his bands against each other - I didn't know. What I did know was that he sold a reasonable number of records for his bands, and I knew we'd never be on his label. He'd made it clear that he thought we were entertaining, but not enough for him to spend his money releasing our records.

While we were loading out after the gig, I stopped to watch the Hippie trying to coax a stray cat out from underneath the Nova. He had a feline fetish; he actually carried a little baggie of cat food around with him in case emergencies such as this arose. He finally got the cat halfway out from under the car. It sniffed around suspiciously, then started wolfing down the food. The Hippie tried to pick up the stray while it was still eating. The cat bit him on the thumb and gave him a long, deep scratch down his forearm before taking off. I couldn't help laughing.

He put us up at his cat-infested house in San Francisco, settling down on the couch with a bag of pot while we laid out our sleeping bags.

The Hippie liked arguing. Everything was a potential debate, be it the political issues of the day or a dust mite. I had nothing to lose by arguing with him, but I kept the personal attacks to a minimum. After all, the guy was giving us a place to stay for the night. We drank beer while he smoked joint after joint of sensemillia.

We finally fell asleep, drunk and happy, at five a.m. I woke up at nine to find the bottom half of my sleeping bag covered in cat piss.

We showered, found a diner and ate breakfast and then drove to the club in San Francisco for our matinee gig. Reverend Dave was pacing on the sidewalk in front of the club. Reverend Dave - back when he'd been in a punk band he'd been known simply as "Dave" - had done a little too much acid over the years and he'd gone a little crazy. He was shouting Bible verses at everyone who walked in the club. Some of them looked like they wanted to stop and punch him. After sobering up and getting religion, he'd gone on a one-man crusade to clean up the neighborhood. He'd singled out a small time drug-dealing punk - the guy was no saint, but Dave had been copping from him only a year before - and tried to turn the other punks against him. When that failed, he found a photo of the dealer and made up fliers condemning him as an evil corrupter of children. He handed the fliers out at shows and posted them in the guy's neighborhood. That had riled up some of the neighbors briefly but Dave wasn't satisfied. He finally called the cops on the guy and ratted him out. The cops found the dealer sitting at home with entirely too much speed in his possession for recreational use. He was currently serving a short term in a prison in the central part of the state.

When I passed by Reverend Dave, he started preaching something about accepting Christ as my savior, consulting his beat-up old bible and stammering over the words.

"Dude, cut it out," I said. "Why don't you back to writing dumb little songs like you used to?"

"You'd like that, wouldn't you?" he said through squinted eyes. "You'd like me to go back to being a speed freak, a junkie, a alcoholic."

"*An* alcoholic. And no, I just wish you'd stop annoying the shit out of everybody."

"That's what punk's supposed to be about. Stirring shit up. That's what I'm doing."

"Punk's not about stirring shit up. It's about three chords and a bad attitude."

" Maybe you oughta think about why you sold out, Joe."

"Dave, I have three dollars to my name. If I've sold out, where's the money?"

But he was already busy harassing another poor bastard who'd made the mistake of crossing his path.

****

The promoter at the Santa Cruz gig screwed us on the door money, so Vic grabbed everything from the club that wasn't nailed down, which meant that we left a few ashtrays and cocktail glasses richer. I made a new rule, Band Rule Number 47: no more dealing with promoters who we hadn't confirmed as being at least semi-honest by other bands or promoters. We promised to give some girl a ride to our next gig in Phoenix in exchange for twenty bucks. She claimed to be a certified massage therapist. Said she'd be happy to work on us for free.

SEVEN

I didn't fuck the Mexican massage therapist. I didn't fuck the peep show stripper either. We met her in Mesa while we were standing outside the record store - the one where the promoter worked - waiting for it to open. Long, black hair cut Betty Page-style, a red miniskirt and fishnet stockings and I was already hard when she said she'd see us at the show that night.

A hundred and ten degrees and no promoter. Eleven-thirty in the morning. We would've been there sooner but we kept having to pull over and let the Nova cool down. We'd driven all night from California and when the sun rose so did the heat. And so did the tempers. Sitting in the shade of the car on the shoulder of I-10, arguing and fucking with each other.

"Hey, Kid, watch out for the rattlesnakes."

"There ain't any rattlensakes out here."

"Of course there are. This is where they come from."

"Really?" A brief look of concern crossed his face. "Nah, you're just fuckin' with me."

"Jimmy, would you tell him there's rattlesnakes out here."

"I don't wanna.. yeah, they live in the desert but I'm not involved in this conversation."

"They sneak up on you," said Vic. "All you hear is the rattle, then *wham*! You're fuckin' dead!"

"If you stand still," said the massage therapist, "they usually won't bite. They only bite when they're provoked."

"No, no no," I said. "That's scorpions."

"I grew up in the desert. I know."

"Well, you know wrong. I'm just trying to look out for The Kid. Band business, if you don't mind."

"Scorpions?" said The Kid, sounding a little scared.

"Where the fuck do you think they come from, the North Pole?"

We really were a bunch of idiots. But hey, it was fun watching The Kid, his eyes darting around like crazy. This was his first tour; he'd never been out of the Midwest in his life. And it served a purpose. He was so afraid of a scorpion crawling into his shoe that he kept his Chuck Taylors on for the rest of the ride, for which everyone was thankful.

When we got into town we spent some time in an air-conditioned Dunkin' Donuts drinking ice water, and we killed some more time inside the air-conditioned record store pretending to shop. The promoter, the guy behind the counter informed us, had the day off. He gave us the promoter's address and after driving around in the heat for an hour and a half we finally found his house. Nobody answered the door. We camped out on the porch, in the shade. When he finally got home, we loaded our stuff into the living room. Vic went out to the Nova, shoeless, to get his bag. He started jumping around on the blacktop, yelling his head off about how hot it was. I was real close to snapping his neck, with the heat and all. Jimmy calmed the punk down before I beheaded him for slamming the Nova's trunk up and down in a frustrated, spastic attempt to shut it while he hopped around wildly like a cartoon character.

The Circle Jerks were playing a gig in town that night, so our warehouse gig got moved to a starting time of 1:30 A.M., which meant we'd hit the stage at around three. We'd be lucky if the soundman stuck around to hear our set. At least the promoter got us passes to the Circle Jerks show.

For most of the Circle Jerks show I hung around outside talking to the peep show stripper but I was on my best behavior; just a little flirting.

In retrospect, I should've tried to fuck her.

I kept calling Sylvia every chance I got but she kept hanging up on me. It's kinda hard to repair a relationship when you're two thousand miles away. And drunk.

****

I'd met Sylvia the first night the band ever played. Some kid's folks' basement, playing mostly cover songs. I guess she was impressed. Saw a guy with a bad attitude; somebody to piss off her parents. She'd just turned sixteen, the perfect age to bring a fuck-up like me home to meet mom. Of course, her mother hated me.

"She says you're a lot like my father," she'd said.

"Oh yeah?"

"I hate my father. You're not like him."

I hoped not. The guy sold insurance for a living.

"Listen," I said, with the worldly wisdom of a seventeen year-old know-it-all. "She's just worried about you. I don't blame her. But she's wrong. I'm not your father."

"I know," she said. But after a while, every time we'd get into a fight, she'd tell me I was just like him. It was an accusation I couldn't defend since I'd never met the guy. Sylvia never talked about him.

What I did know was that the old man finally smacked Syliva's mom around in a drunken rage one time too many. After they'd gotten divorced Sylvia had lived in an apartment in Oak Lawn with her mom and her aunt for a few years until her mom married Dwayne. Sylvia had never spoken to her father after the divorce. She never told me why and I stopped asking after a couple of years. I figured he'd probably smacked her around too, maybe molested her. Which didn't speak too highly of me if I was supposed to be just like him.

****

I called her every few days but she wasn't home much and when she was she always sounded preoccupied, distant at best. I couldn't really blame her but I did anyway. She'd been loyal - I'd been fucking anything that moved. But I loved the girl. I think I did. It's hard to remember now. But I'm pretty sure I loved her, and being away from home and drunk, I felt sorry for myself. And it kinda felt good, even knowing that she was probably out fucking somebody else. Hell, that made it better. I'd changed my ways; I'd been good, for almost three weeks now. She was acting irrationally; she was making too big a deal out of it. Sure, I'd fucked around on her and I knew logically I'd hurt her but what had really swung it for me was that I'd felt terrible whenever I'd stopped to think about it. Christ, that's why I'd finally spilled my guts; my Catholic upbringing rearing its ugly head again. So I fucked up, but it was over now. Why couldn't she just grow up? But I knew her, and I knew she had to get even.

EIGHT

The Kid was having his own problems with his girlfriend, and as a result he was being a dick to everyone - uncommunicative most of the time and whiny the rest. Fuck him - I had enough to deal with without concerning myself with his love life. Half our records had succumbed to the desert heat in Arizona. I don't know why none of us had been bright enough to take them out of the carrier, but when we pulled the merch out before the Houston gig, we found an entire box of records that were warped to the point where all we could do was throw them in the nearest dumpster. There went two hundred and fifty bucks.

We stayed in an abandoned house just outside Houston. It was some kid's mother's house but they didn't live there anymore.

"Why not?" I asked on the way there.

"Well, part of it kinda burned down."

By the time we arrived, it was raining. It was a real dorky suburban house - like the Brady Bunch in Texas. After a tornado. Since half the roof was gone, we all had to stay in the living room. The bathroom was already flooded with a few inches of water and the toilet didn't work. The living room carpet was moist and the floor was covered with what looked like chicken feathers and pages ripped from the Satanic

Bible. Jimmy and I couldn't figure out if the stains on the carpet were blood and we didn't want to get close enough to find out.

We'd met a couple of girls after the gig and they'd followed us in their car. Jimmy was getting friendly with one of them. The other one sat talking with me and The Kid. Vic was slouched in a chair, drunk, a blink or two away from a blissful alcoholic slumber. He always managed to exude an aura of cool, even when he was asleep. The guy really seemed to live a charmed life. He wasn't the sharpest knife in the drawer and he wasn't the best looking punk rocker at the show but he always got the chicks and he always ended up landing on his feet even when the rest of us were sitting on our asses, bruised and confused.

"Good turnout tonight," said The Kid.

"Yeah," I said. "I guess this is a good town for punk rock."

"*Yeah* it is," said the girl in that Southern way of accenting the "yeah," like she was disagreeing with you. "Nirvana is playing next week."

"Oh yeah," I answered. "I think I've heard them. They're not really a punk band though. In fact, they kinda suck."

She was instantly furious.

"I *like* Nirvana. They're better than your band."

I hadn't noticed how ugly she was. Long hair in dreadlocks, unwashed, most likely, for months. Blemishes all over her face. A nose ring covered with snot from her constantly dripping snout.

"Fuck them. We'd blow their scurvy hippie asses off the stage anytime, anywhere."

"You wish."

"That's your best comeback? Jesus, I gave that one up in the seventh grade."

"Why is he such an asshole?" she asked Jimmy. He didn't answer. He was busy with his new friend.

"Lighten up. If you like 'em that's your problem."

"Well I *do* like them."

"Okay, princess. You wanna like shitty bands, be my guest."

"You're a fuckhead."

"You're a dingbat," said the Kid.

"Fuck you, you scrawny little shit."

"Watch out, Kid," I said. "These dykes can be pretty tough."

"Fuck you both. I'm getting out of here."

"Bye."

"Jackie, let's go."

Jackie's tongue was deep inside Jimmy's mouth. She wasn't going anywhere.

"Don't look at me," I said.

"So I have to stay here with you two assholes?"

"Go sleep in the backyard, dummy," said The Kid.

"Or you could just walk home," I offered.

"It's twenty miles."

"So maybe you can work off that spare tire you're sporting."

"Someday somebody's gonna kick the shit out of you and shut your big mouth."

"It's already happened. It only made me louder."

I finally got bored with playing with her so I grabbed my sleeping bag and announced that I was going to sleep in the car. The Kid came with me. I took the backseat; he curled up in the front. I sat there smoking cigarettes, listening to the rain and The Kid. The Kid was a little worked up. He was going on and on about what a cunt the Nirvana girl was and how we'd put her down good. That kind of stuff was always fun for him. For me too, but I don't know if The Kid realized how dumb it all was. At least it had gotten him out of his pissy mood for the time being.

The next morning we drove back into Houston and got an oil change, then hit the Denny's next door for breakfast. After I ordered, I made for the pay phone and called Sylvia.

"You should stop calling me," she said.

"What? Why?"

"I don't wanna see you anymore. I can do better than you."

"No you can't. Nobody'll treat you as good as I do."

"You arrogant prick! Who the fuck do you think you are?"

"The best boyfriend a wingnut like you will ever be lucky enough to find. And the only guy dumb enough to put up with your temper tantrums and all your other crazy bullshit."

"Do you really think any other girl would put up with *your* shit?"

"I know it."

"You're a fuckin' wacko. I don't have to listen to you anymore. Why am I having this conversation with you? We're broken up! I *dumped* you! I already told you I can do better than you."

"Oh yeah? Good luck!"

I slammed down the phone, went back to the booth and looked at the stack of pancakes in front of me. I stubbed my cigarette out in the melting pile of butter on the top. I wasn't hungry.

We had to drive to San Antonio for the next gig. We'd routed the tour as best we could, but we still ended up playing a gig, going hundreds of miles west for the next one, then passing through the town we'd played the night before on the way to the next gig a few more hundred miles *east*. Jimmy was driving, so I amused myself by pulling out a marker and a big photo of Sylvia - one that had been taken for her senior year of high school - and spending about an hour carefully blacking out most of her teeth, drawing in flies dropping from her hair, fumes coming from her armpits, a hairy upper lip, crossed eyeballs, the works. When I was finished I passed it back to Vic.

"Whoah, dude," he said, "That's insane."

"No," I answered. "I'm just getting out a little aggression in a harmless way. Some might call it productive."

"I don't know, man. That's kinda weird, spending all that time to do that."

I didn't say anything. But I did feel just a little bit insane.

****

The San Antonio gig was a bust. The promoter was a Puerto Rican nazi skinhead who apparently saw no contradictions between his heritage and his socio-political beliefs. He had us booked on a bill with three speedmetal bands who offered to "loan" us their gear: fifty bucks for the bass amp, thirty for each guitar amp, a hundred for the drums. We bailed without playing and made the trip to New Orleans.

Susie, the promoter, let us stay at her house. She even promised to get me laid. She took us out on the town and showed us the sights. We sampled beer at the local microbrewery and visited a voodoo shop where I picked up a candle that would put a curse on Sylvia.

Susie made us crawfish, corn on the cob and new potatoes for dinner, all washed down with plenty of Busch. When we got to the show I immediately checked out the female situation and put the cutest girl - a little blond headed Madonna look alike - on the guest list. When she got to the door and discovered she didn't have to pay, I gave her my kindest drunken leer and said, "I put you on the list."

"Thanks," she answered, as she moved to get the hell away from me.

The show was great - we'd drawn about a hundred and fifty people. No fights, no problems with the sound. "Suck My Pussy" went over really well even though none of the fans had ever heard it before. By the middle of the song they were slamming around in the pit like crazy. You had to appreciate nights like that.

After the show, Susie paid Jimmy and introduced me to the girl she'd found for me. Cuntosauraus. The girl would've just as soon chopped my dick off as look at me. We spent most of the night arguing. I briefly wondered if I was starting to argue with random girls just to remind me of being with Sylvia. Same pointless, bitchy arguments filled with plenty of nasty insults and personal attacks. Or maybe I was just a prick. I mean, who's a prick going to end up hanging out with other than a loud mouthed bitch? I didn't have the temperament or personality to attract sane, decent girls.

The next morning, me and The Kid were dispatched to drive The Cunt to work. Jimmy was going through the merch and door money with the calculator and Vic was still passed out from a night of too many beers with a stripper he'd met after the show. The Cunt bitched and moaned about my driving and bitched and moaned about being late for work and bitched and moaned about my attitude and my hangover got worse and worse until I finally pulled over at a gas station and ordered her out.

"Fuck you," she said. "You're giving me a ride to work."

"You fuckin' shithead, I'll put a tire iron upside your head if you don't start walking."

She got out. The Kid applauded me and we drove back to Susie's.

****

The next night we played a skate park in Jacksonville. The skater kids were pissed at me and The Kid 'cause we made fun of them. They were even more pissed when we were dispatched to judge the skate contest before the gig because we had the temerity to give first prize to the funniest skater rather than the one who was technically the best. They all skated to the newest album from the latest straight-edge sensation out of New York. There was a kid who didn't know his ass from a hole in the ground, and knew it, and was just making a fool of himself on the skateboard. He was entertaining. Reminded me of our band; not knowing what we were doing, no real talent, but doing it anyway just for the hell of it. So we gave him first prize. The promoter overturned our decision and gave the prize to some snot who didn't appreciate us. He took his prize - a copy of our second album - and cracked it in half. The skaters hated us, so of course it was a fun show. I endlessly capped on the New York band - they were going to be playing the next night - while onstage, to plenty of shouts of "fuck you" and "you suck," the eternal cries of the wit-impaired punk.

We left a note with the promoter for the New York band. It was written by The Kid with a little input from me. It read:

Dear Pussies:
We'll kick your straight edge asses any day of the week. You dick-smokers aren't man enough to hold our jockstraps. If you're ever unlucky enough to get in our way, we'll spank you and take away your shiny guitars.
Fuck You,
Pagan Icons

The promoter promised he'd deliver the message.

We slept at his girlfriend's apartment that night. She was only sixteen but she'd managed to move out of her mom's, get a full time job and rent an apartment. We went swimming in one of the five pools in the complex.

A cute young girl named Promise, one of our host's friend's, had been giving me the eye all night. I was going to swim over to the other end of the pool to work my charms when she started kissing some goofy punk kid. I could see his hand under the water working inside the crotch of her shorts.

I was up half the night listening to her get fucked in the back room.

The next morning, her friends told me that the local punk boys all treated their girlfriends like shit until a band came through town - then they acted all nice so the girls wouldn't go out and have some fun. Lousy little punks.

****

Twenty-four hours later, I found myself standing in front of a mic in a backyard in Tampa at a house party with a two dollar cover, playing songs for twenty nazi skinheads and a handful of punks. The skins were dancing around in a circle; smashing anyone who got in their way; sig-heiling us and chanting "Pa-Gan-I-Cons!" over and over. We were cursed with a band name that worked perfectly for moronic chants by people who could only string together four syllables at a time. Pleased as I was to be winning over the white power faction, I couldn't help feeling a little unsettled. Skinheads were bad enough, always creating a menacing tone, but with the Nazis things *always* ended in violence. When the next door neighbor started yelling "fascists!" at them and they threw lawn chairs at her, I knew it was gonna get ugly. They finally jumped a punk and started pounding on him. I threw my guitar behind me and joined the fracas, which was already over by the time I got there. The punk wasn't hurt too bad.

That pretty much ended the party. Most of the skins left, tossing M-80's at the house as they walked away. A few of them stayed, and I got into an idiotic debate with them about race and the place of the ignorant, backwards black man in our fine nation and the evil Jewish cabal that controlled the world's banking system and Aryan superiority and all that crazy bullshit. Drunk and loose. Trying to talk sense to the senseless. Somehow I managed to keep from getting pummeled.

The Kid and Jimmy crashed out on the living room floor, and the girl having the party showed us her bedroom, where she said me and Vic could sleep. She was taking the couch. Me and Vic were still awake and kinda wired, so we brought a twelve pack of Busch out to the car and I grabbed my Fender and sat down on the trunk, drinking and playing tunes for a couple of punks who were still hanging around, Vic keeping time by beating the palms of his hands against his Levi-encased thighs. There was a nazi girl sitting alone against the side of the house, drinking a Busch and listening to the tunes. The punks left when I ran out of tunes. Vic walked off with one of the punk girls and the rest of the beer.

I put the guitar in the trunk and walked over to the nazi girl. She was pretty cute: she had that short bowl haircut with the long bangs and sides, and she wore a green bomber with American flags and swastika patches and such bullshit sewn on, and black jeans and red Doc Martens. She was drunk. And bored.

"The evening is winding down," I said, not having any idea what I was talking about.

She just looked at me, cool; "I don't give a fuck" written all over her face, but trying a little too hard.

"Got any more beer?" I asked. She handed me the can and I took a long sip and gave it back to her. I sat down across from her, on the driveway. To my right I could see a skinhead and a punk rocker leaning against a fence next to the garage, sharing a joint. There was a security light on the side of the garage; from the chest down they might've had a spotlight on them.

"I don't have a ride home," said the skin girl. "Gotta wait for him." She hooked her thumb in the direction of the skinhead.

"Oh." I was really turning on the charm.

"I'm Joe," I said, sticking out my hand for her to shake, like an idiot. She just looked at it. So cool I almost laughed.

"I know," she said. She finished her beer and tossed the can behind her and then pulled a pack of Marlboros from her jacket and lit one, really turning up the bored as hell look. I asked her for her lighter and fired up a Kool.

"Those are nigger smokes," she said.

"I'm a nigger lover," I answered, throwing the lighter back to her. "I like spics too. The Kid has a Puerto Rican girlfriend. He says Hispanic girls have better smelling pussies."

"Bullshit," she snorted, as she started unlacing her boots. "They don't shower."

"I never fucked one."

"They're the scum of society."

"You're a foulmouthed little slut. Why don't you act like a human being?"

"Hey smart-ass, my boyfriend's standing right over there," she said, pointing to the garage, where it appeared the skinhead was whispering to the punk. In his ear.

46

"You better call him over before he gets too busy."

She flicked her cigarette at me and then pulled her Docs off and tossed them at me halfheartedly.

"You look like a dago."

"No, I'm a kraut, potato-eating, bagpipe-playing, wooden-shoe-wearing proud American."

"Fucking fag."

"Your boyfriend's got a dick in his mouth," I noted, which was actually true at the moment. We watched the skin suck the punk's dick. The punk was smacking the skin with the back of his hand. Occasionally, he'd take hold of the belt on his leather jacket and hit the skin in the face with the buckle.

"You wanna fuck?" she asked, pulling down the zipper on her pants. What did I have to lose? Only my self-respect and I didn't have a hell of a lot of that left anyway.

She took her jeans off, then her panties, and laid her bomber down so the jacket was protecting her ass from the lawn. Then she pulled up her t-shirt and tossed it to the side. I pulled my sneakers and pants off but I left my t-shirt on. I got down between her legs and licked my way up her thighs until I smelled pussy. I grabbed her by the waist and pulled her pussy up to meet my face. I looked up, my tongue on her clit, and saw the sheen of sweat on her chest, saw her hard little nipples straining up like they were about to burst, saw her eyes fixated on her boyfriend. I lifted my head to follow her stare. The skin was bent over, his fingers laced into the chain link fence, getting it in the ass from the punk.

I brought my head back down and sucked her clit into my mouth, hard, sucking on it with as much pressure as I could, using my teeth a little. She was breathing faster, and her leg muscles were clenching up, and she was trying not to scream when I used my teeth. Her head was still turned towards her boyfriend. We could hear him moaning and begging to be fucked harder, faster, like a chick in a porno flick.

I got up and rested on my knees, then pushed my dick inside her, grabbing her by the ankles to spread her legs apart more. I fucked her until I felt like I was going to cum, then I pulled out and let my dick jerk around in the air, just one touch away from exploding.

"Fucking nigger," she hissed. "Dago nigger! Fucking wop!"

"Shut the fuck up, whore. I told you I'm not Italian." I fucked her for as long as I could, stopping and waiting when I felt I was going to cum. I must've done it ten times. My balls were starting to ache. Over by the garage, the punk seemed to cum inside the skin's ass. The punk pulled up his jeans and the skin stood up, pants still around his ankles. He started stroking his dick.

I moved up to her chest until the tip of my dick was at her lips. She sucked it, simultaneously pissed off and aroused. Her boyfriend stroked his hard prick; it was plainly visible in the bright light shining down from the side of the garage.

"I'm gonna cum," I said, and she pulled her head away a little and jacked me off. I shot all over her face, her lips, her nose, her eyes. Cum landed on her cheeks, on her forehead, in her hair, and at the same time, we watched as her boyfriend shot a load all over the driveway, hips thrusting in time with mine, shooting his cum as far as I shot mine. I pulled my jeans back up as the skin pulled his up.

I left his girlfriend laying on the grass, sweating, limp, sticky, looking like she'd been raped, and I felt a sick kind of satisfaction.

Me and Vic slept together that night in the promoter's bedroom. Her boyfriend had custom-built the bed for her - it was up on a loft - and it was built for a very short girl. We scrunched up and managed to catch a few winks between half-awake bouts of shoving each other onto the floor.

The next day Annie Mah came by to tell us she'd taken some good photos of us at the party the night before, and to take us to a laundromat. One of the nazi skinheads - he couldn't have been older than fourteen - had followed her, wanting to hang out with us. We walked over to the laundromat and threw our clothes and a little shampoo into two machines. I went to the sink in the back of the room and dyed my mohawk blue again; it had started to fade. I hadn't shaved the sides of my head in a week, so I pulled my razor out of my bag and got the warm water running. The skin came over and offered to shave the back for me. He wasn't going to make much of a skinhead with an attitude like that.

NINE

We drove up to Atlanta and played a Knights Of Columbus hall in the suburbs. The promoter bought us a keg of Busch and dragged it into the backstage area, which was really just an office. A girl with long, blonde hair came in. She wasn't fat, but she was close. I knew this because she came over and sat on my lap. A buck thirty-five at least and if she cut her hair she'd look like something that just hopped off a lilypad. I told her to go away, and she pouted as she left the room.

By the time we hit the stage I was blasted. I immediately stripped down to my boxers.

"You fuckin' hayseeds can suck my dick!" I yelled into the mic. Nobody said anything. Just stared, like Aunt Bea casting a wary eye at a drunken Otis.

"You stump-jumping, sister-fucking, rednecked hicks, I'll piss on your graves!"

I climbed up the speaker stack and grabbed onto a steel beam on the ceiling with my right hand. I hung there, an easy target, the mic in my left hand.

"I'm a fuckin' monkey," I said. I noticed some skinheads in the back of the room.

"Which one of you baldheaded faggots wants to come up here and blow me?" I asked innocently. I dropped to the stage and pulled my boxers down. "Come on up and suck it." My dick was trying to retreat inside my body, shrivelling up like a miniature Slinky as if it knew it was being gaped at. One of the skins shouted, "Fuck you, homo!"

Jimmy leaned over to The Kid's mic.

"If that was a chick up here," he said, "you'd all be fighting for a front row seat." Which was true enough. But the skin didn't like that. He rushed the stage, fist back. Jimmy was about to get hit hard. Two bouncers stepped over to the middle of the stage, casually, and grabbed the skin. He was escorted outside.

"What the fuck is that?" I asked into the mic, pointing at a haggard old grey-haired broad wearing a beat up leather jacket.

"She used to date Joey Ramone!" somebody yelled.

I pulled up my piss-stained skivvies, grabbed my crotch and strapped on my guitar. "Ahhh, bullshit," I said, and the band kicked into the first song. Joey Ramone's ex-girlfriend threw an empty bottle of Smirnoff at me. I ducked and it missed me. See, now that I wasn't drinking Bud, my dick was getting hard and my reflexes were right on...

After our set, I went back to the keg and Blondie came back to sit on my lap. This time she was greeted by a hard dick trying to poke a hole through my jeans. Fuck looks, fuck weight, I was horny. It wasn't like we were getting married. We kissed for a while, then me and the boys loaded out the gear and headed for the house where we were staying - some rich kid whose folks were on vacation in Belize. Blondie and her friend Elaine came along. Elaine and Vic were already exploring each other's tongues in the back seat.

We got to the house and discovered it was a small mansion. The kid putting us up had made a lame attempt to have a party - show off that he was pals with the band even though we didn't know him and didn't really care to - but we weren't interested. Watching a bunch of jerks trying to impress you with their drunken antics, trying to out-punk each other by acting like ten-year olds while pretending like they didn't even notice you were sitting there was a scene we'd witnessed too many times before. We made small talk in pig latin amongst ourselves, letting Vic do most of the talking. He was an expert in pig latin; he talked so quickly and with so much confidence that it sounded like he was speaking French. Between the pig latin and the four of us yawning loudly and in unison, the kid finally kicked his friends out and went upstairs to bed with his girlfriend. Jimmy and The Kid camped out in the living room, Vic and Elaine went to the den, and me and Blondie went down the hall to the guest room on the ground floor.

"Ukfay emay," she said, laughing.

"I think we can drop the pig latin now, doll."

She pushed me onto the bed and gave me sloppy, drunken head, but when I tried to go down on her, she said, "No. No oral sex in this house. Onay ayway." I didn't bother trying to figure her out. I satisfied myself by playing around with her gigantic tits; it took me about a half hour just to get her bra off. It was, like, specially made to hold up those enormous jugs.

I finally climbed on top of her and stuck it in.

"Slow down, big boy," she said. I hadn't noticed how dry she was. I licked my fingers and rubbed them around her lips, pushing a finger inside. She was a real blonde. I took my finger out and slid my dick in slowly. I was pretty wasted so I wasn't too hard.

Busch is made by the same company that makes Budweiser. Maybe I'd have to switch beers again...

I came inside the rubber I'd been wise enough to put on and headed to the bathroom, where I sat down on the toilet and expelled a torrential blast of diarrhea. I wiped my ass, lit a Kool and crept over to the den. Elaine had her face buried in Vic's crotch. She was alternating between sucking his dick and trying to talk him into putting a rubber on. He was working as hard as he could to convince her that a rubber wasn't needed. And then a flashlight shined in the window, a huge picture window that took up most of the wall.

"Yo!" I yelled, a little louder than I'd meant to. I dropped to the floor.

There was a knock on the window. Vic and Elaine had hit the deck too; they were just barely underneath the window. I slinked back to the bedroom and turned out the light.

"What's going on?" asked Blondie.

"I don't know."

A couple of minutes passed, then the doorbell rang. Blondie peeked out the window.

"It's the cops," she said.

"How old are you?" I asked.

"Fifteen."

"Oh, shit. I'm fucked."

"Get a hold of yourself," she said, suddenly all serious and mature. She pulled on her shirt and pants and walked down the hall. I followed her. She opened the door, with me standing right behind it, peeking through the crack in the door at the guy who might at any moment be booking me for statutory rape.

"Sorry to bother you," said the cop. "We're looking for Elaine Cummings. Her parents think she might be here."

"Who?"

"Elaine Cummings."

"I've never heard of her. Sorry."

"You haven't seen any teenage girls here?"

"No," said Blondie. "What time is it? My husband has to get up for work in the morning."

"Sorry," said the cop. "If you see a teenage girl around here, call the police department."

"I'm not going to see *anyone*. I'm going back to bed." They both kind of chuckled, as if that was funny.

"Sorry I couldn't help you."

"Thanks anyway," said the cop. And he and his partner just left. It made no sense but I didn't need it to. They were gone and they weren't coming back and I wasn't going to spend the rest of the night in a redneck jail cell.

We went back to the bedroom and Blondie climbed on top of me and fucked me again. Afterwards, as I was putting my sweatpants on, I asked her, "You're sure you're only fifteen?"

"Yeah."

Well, the cop was fooled too, so I didn't feel so bad.

****

The next day as we were piling into the car, Jimmy leaned over to me.

"That chick you were with last night came into the bathroom while I was taking a shower this morning."

"Oh yeah?"

"She asked me if I wanted to fuck her."

"Yeah, I think she's nuts."

She was. Unfortunately, we had to stay in town for another day 'cause we didn't have a gig that night. She followed us around for the rest of the day, acting like a mental case, really getting a kick out of annoying the hell out of me. We ended up getting invited to stay in an enormous college dorm room by a punk we met at a Burger King. The boys sat around playing video games in the living room. I spent most of the night trying to talk the crazy bitch out of the bathroom.

"Come on out."

"Jo-oe-oey! *Jo-Jo*! You're being *mean* to me."

"I'll fucking *show* you mean!"

"I'm gonna slit my wrists."

"Fuck, don't do that."

And so on. I finally talked her out of the can, and she said she was sorry and that she was going to go home. I almost got her to the front door of the building, but she stopped by the stairwell.

"Kiss me," she said.

"No."

"Plee-ee-a-se!"

"For fuck's sake, go home!"

She tried to hug me. I pushed her away.

"Fuck me," she said.

"No way."

"Come on!" She started pulling her pants down. A couple of students walked down the stairs, saw us and started walking faster.

"You're a fuckin' embarrassment. Get the fuck outta here."

She pulled her pants back up. "I'm gonna kill myself."

"Good. Need any help?"

She started making crying noises, hitching her shoulders up and jerking around; the worst acting job I'd seen since the last Melanie Griffith movie. She put the tips of her forefingers above her forehead, then brought them around her face to the bottom of her chin, making an imaginary circle. She scrunched up her forehead and drew her lips downward in a pouty frown.

"I'm so sad," she said. "Why am I so sad?"

"Because you're fuckin' certifiable."

"No, it's the world. The world makes me sad."

"You make me sick. Why don't you beat it."

She finally got bored with the game and turned to leave. I followed her just outside the door and watched her walk away. When she reached the road, she turned around and yelled, "I'm sorry!" Then she started laughing like crazy and ran off.

As we were loading our bags into the car the next morning, I said loudly "New Band Rule!"

Everybody groaned and started to protest.

"No, this one's mostly for me. No more banging crazy chicks on the road. Band Rule Number 59."

Nobody complained.

****

I started drinking Bud again. I wrote a new song to commemorate it:

Miller's the Champagne of beers, King Cobra's fucking cheap
And Schaefer's fine but of them all
Budweiser's the King Of Beers I drink it every night
'Cause I'm in love with alcohol

99 bottles of beer are on the wall
But the party's only starting so I say
We're going to the store and we're gonna get some more
We'll break down the bedroom door then we'll pass out on the floor

It's funny how I always wake up thinking to myself
This really isn't any fun
I've got a killer of a headache and my mouth is always dry
And I'm only twenty-one

And I swear I'll never ever touch another beer again
But then the evening rolls around
And I drink and piss so much that I think I'm gonna drown
And when I finally find the bed the room is spinning round and round

I was really at my peak. The voice of a generation.

****

The last few shows had been cancelled so we all voted to give up and go back home - cut our losses. The morning we got back, I dropped the guys off and drove straight to Sylvia's. I waited outside for a couple hours until she got back from work. She didn't look happy to see me, but she didn't seem all that pissed, either. She had something up her sleeve or else she would've laid me out right there on the street. We went inside and I started to tell her I was sorry and all that, and she told me to shut up. I shut up.

She went down the hall for a few minutes. When she came back she was barefoot. She sat on the couch.

"Suck my toes," she said.

"What?"

"You heard me."

"Listen..."

"Shut up and suck my toes."

I started sucking them. Her feet smelled awful. She was enjoying it, watching me humiliate myself. When she'd had enough, she stood up, turned around and pulled up her skirt.

"Fuck me."

I stood up and fucked her. As soon as she came, she pulled away and sat back down on the couch.

"If you wanna jack off on my feet, you can," she said.

Of course I did.

TEN

I promised Sylvia I'd meet her at Mary's Fourth of July party out in the suburbs - a few miles from Sylvia's mom's house. I brought Vic with for moral support - I could usually count on him. Vic could drink a case of beer and you'd never be able to tell. He was always sort of in his own little world; cool, relaxed, confident, laid-back. I worried about his drinking - he was worse than me - but he always showed up for rehearsal and he was always prepared for recordings and gigs. I didn't have to baby-sit him. And in times of potential conflict he was good to have around; he always backed me up, even when I was dead wrong. Potential conflict usually involved a pissed off punk wanting to pound my face but I figured he'd work just as well as a buffer between me and Sylvia if things got crazy.

We were sitting out back on the patio, Sylvia giving me the evil eye. When she got a wild hair across her ass you had to watch out. She was a vindictive little thing. I was drinking, but not too much to do or say anything stupid. I was done with Bud, King Cobra and Busch. I stuck to 16-ounce Old Style's. When one of Sylvia's friends started yammering away about the evils of corporate America and the superiority of the Cuban government - fuckin' *Cuba* for chrissakes - I resisted the urge to light the pack of firecrackers I had in my back pocket and throw 'em at her. I just nodded my head and smiled, pretending I was lobotomized. Kelly Castro was too busy listening to the sound of her own voice to realize I was mocking her, which was for the best.

Sylvia went in the house for something, and some blonde-headed dingbat who looked like the top of a cheerleading squad pyramid immediately started putting the moves on me. I went around to the side of the house to piss. The Blonde came over and watched me pee.

"Beat it," I told her.

I buttoned my jeans and went back to the patio to wait for Sylvia. I drank two more beers before I finally went into the house and looked around for her. I made my way upstairs to the bedrooms. One of the doors was closed. I opened it. It was unlocked, naturally. She was on her knees in front of some big dope on the bed, sucking his dick.

He took one look at me and pulled away from her.

"It wasn't me!" he yelled. "It was her, she was all over me."

I just looked at him. He bailed out. And she started cussing me out, which I thought was ludicrous since the whole thing had been set up so I'd bust her. She was always so obvious. I walked downstairs, calmly, and she followed me, screaming her goddamned head off. I walked through the front door and out into the yard. She was still following me, making a soap opera out of our lives for the benefit of thirty other drunks.

"Joe Pagan, big fuckin' rock star with his stupid little band, fucking all the dumb punk girls. You think you're such hot shit!"

"No, I really..."

"Well nobody gives a *fuck* about you..."

"Certainly not you..."

"...because you treat everybody like *shit*! You fuck! You fucking *fuckhead*!"

"I'm not the one who just had a dick in my mouth."

She kicked me in the balls. She kept hitting me and kicking me, and ripping at my t-shirt, crying, screaming over and over, "It's not fair!" I just stood there and took it.

She finally got tired of yelling at me and started walking home. I drove Vic back to his apartment and then went back over to Don's.

When Don got home, he told me the he was broke and the label was going under. He was drunk and crying. I couldn't stand looking at him.

"Have another beer," I told him.

I moved out the next day and me and Jimmy quit the label a week later. I had to smile at the thought of quitting a job that we'd never been paid for. Christ, we were pitiful.

****

I moved my three couch cushions into the ShitHole and took to drinking more, until I'd run out of money. Then I'd sit in my room on the middle cushion and stare at the turned off TV, trying not to think of anything. When it worked, I'd sit there for a long time, not thinking, not doing anything, just sitting. I always felt good after doing it. Sometimes somebody would stomp by the door and ask what I was doing.

"Drinking deeply from the well of my soul," I'd say, or some such garbage.

"Oh," they'd always answer. "You're jerking off."

I got a landscaping gig part time. It was the only work I could stand. Just cutting lawns and trimming bushes, ten hours a day, three, sometimes four days a week. It didn't pay much but there was always money for beer and cigarettes. There wasn't always money for food, but Sylvia and I were still sort of unofficially together despite our constant arguments and she'd steal Ramen and bread and peanut butter from her mother's pantry and bring it to me once a week.

The building that housed the ShitHole had been sold. The new owner wasn't sure what he was ultimately going to do with it, but he gave its illegal tenants a choice: pay rent or get out. The junkies on the second floor left. For five hundred a month, the punks stayed. Damon - the most responsible of us all, which wasn't saying much - signed the lease and was in charge of collecting the rent from everyone and paying the landlord. I only had to come up with seventy-five bucks but I barely made it each month. People moved in and out quickly; the place was always filthy and noisy. Overflowing ashtrays and hundreds of beer cans and bottles littered the floor. Strangers roaming around at all hours. Kicking people I'd never met out of my room, hoping they hadn't gotten cum stains on my couch cushions. Drunk, broke and bored, I'd end up in the dumbest conversations imaginable.

"What came first, the chicken or the egg?" Literally. That was worth three hours.

"I think we should paint that wall black."

"No way, it should be white."

Five hours.

Killing time. Fucking murdering it. Playing pool on a comically warped table with bent cues, none of us even knowing how to play. Trying to keep our few possessions from being stolen by the new group of junkies on the first floor. Putting up every touring band that came through town. Somebody decides to have a last minute party. Somebody's band starts rehearsing at midnight.

"You fuckin' assholes, I gotta get up for work at six!"

"We'll keep it down."

Ramen for breakfast and dinner. Beer for lunch, and whenever else there was time to kill.

It got more depressing when Kara started coming around. Well, Kara had always been around - she was one of the smartest, most sarcastic, fun girls in the scene - but she hadn't always been a junkie. All of a sudden everybody seemed to be snorting heroin. Then shooting it. I didn't like being around it and I didn't like watching my friends kill themselves but Kara was too much for me to take. She'd been so cool. She'd been a step ahead of everybody else for as long as I'd known her. Some punks were funny, but Kara was witty and wit is rare and deserving of respect. And I'd always respected her. When I found her in the alley behind the ShitHole fucking bums for spare change to buy smack, the charm of living in a punk house started to wear off.

****

My older brother had a spare room in his apartment in Roscoe Village and he said I could stay there for a few months. I got a job at the same place Sylvia was working; five hour shifts telemarketing. Selling magazine subscriptions to lonely old ladies. I figured it would give me a chance to get back in good with Sylvia. Show her I could hold a job. She always had a job. Always had a few extra bucks. She was just finishing summer classes at community college, getting ready to go to school in the city. I was still floating around aimlessly.

We fought all the time. Especially when other people were around. We criticized each other constantly. I didn't understand her and she sure didn't understand me. I was starting to get worried that she was leaving me behind. Not that she had any big plans for the future, but at least she was working and going to school. The bad boy charm was wearing thin. She wanted something more, something she wasn't going to get from me. But I loved her. I was pretty goddamn sure I loved her. I didn't know what I'd do without her. I couldn't stand her, but I couldn't stand the thought of not having her. I guess she must've felt the same way about me or she would've dumped me.

So I tried. I really fucking tried. I went in wearing the cleanest shirt I could find, and new Levi's my brother had bought me out of pity. Sweet-talked the boss into giving me a gig - same hours as Sylvia. Reading from a script, shilling lonely people, so lonely they were willing to talk to a telemarketer when they could be watching their "stories" or preparing a noose to hang themselves in their bedrooms.

After about an hour, the manager came over to my cubicle, irritated.

"If they sound black, hang up," he told me. "The blacks'll talk your ear off but you'll never close the deal."

I lasted two days.

It took a while, but things eventually smoothed over. We more or less hated each other's guts but I figured that for reasons beyond our control, me and Sylvia were meant to be together. We fought and fucked, and in between we tried to stay out of each other's way. It was a real punk rock romance.

LOSER

ELEVEN

By the time I was twenty-three, I'd kind of gotten my shit together. Me and Sylvia were living together by then, and our new bassist, Simon, was sharing the apartment with us.

Simon was a pudgy, redheaded kid whose family had moved to Chicago from Scotland when he was still in diapers. He didn't have the thick Scottish accent that his parents did but he talked fast - too fast to keep up with himself. His words tumbled out of his mouth practically on top of one another; he seldom made much sense. He normally wore thick glasses but he occasionally tried to wear contact lenses. The contacts were always making his eyes all runny; they were already usually dark red because he smoked pot incessantly. But the icing on the cake was the haircut; a haircut that almost defied description. The sides and back of his head were cut close to the skull - almost shaved - and the hair that was left was cut mushroom-style, as if a bowl had been placed over his head before the operation. It was the type of low-maintenance haircut normally given to those members of society with such limited mental capacity that they neither know nor care how bad they look. Between the hair, the *High Times* life-style, the runny eyes and the babbling, he was a pitiful, horrible sight to behold. Still, I found him somewhat amusing. The others, particularly Vic, were always on the verge of throwing a blanket over his head and pounding him senseless.

The band had broken up right after I'd moved into the ShitHole. We'd burned out. Gotten tired of losing money and going nowhere. And we'd started getting tired of each other. The Kid quit, and so did Jimmy and that ended it. We kept in touch occasionally, but only because we'd run into each other at shows or parties.

The Nova finally died so I couldn't work anymore - I'd been delivering pizzas along with the landscaping gig and I couldn't do either without a car. My brother got sick of my inability to pay my share of the rent so I gave up and moved in with my folks up in Round Lake Beach for a couple of years. I worked a bunch of shitty temp. jobs, washing dishes, working on an assembly line, finally settling in for a regular gig hauling boxes in a warehouse. Just biding my time, waiting for something to come along.

****

Pagan Icons finally did a reunion show in early 1991 to raise money to pay back the guy who had lent us five hundred bucks to record our second album; the album hadn't made any profit according to Don, so we never got any royalties.

During our set, some skinhead came up to the front of the stage and shoved me in the chest. I shoved him back and the next thing I knew I was on the ground getting pummeled by seven or eight of his buddies, one of whom was jumping up and down on my right foot like crazy. By the time the rest of the band had gotten down there it was over. I hadn't been hurt too badly - even though my foot was throbbing like crazy - so we had the bouncers boot the skinheads and finished our set.

After the show, we all ended up at the bar and, after a few pitchers of beer, decided to get the band back together. After a few more pitchers, we decided that Jimmy would quit the band he was in and we'd take Pagan Icons seriously this time. Vic wanted in, and we wanted him in. The Kid wanted to play in a metal band with his brother so he was out.

I agreed to start up the band again, but only as long as some changes were made. I wanted to do a real band, not some million mile an hour joke designed solely to piss people off and get us laid. Actually write real songs. Tone down the crowd baiting and try to see if we actually had enough talent to hold our own without being a circus act. Everybody else agreed.

A couple of weeks later, I went down to Sylvia's parents' house for dinner, still limping around with a swollen toe. After we ate, I told her to come to the bathroom with me. I sat down on the edge of the bathtub and took off my shoe and my sock. I peeled the blackened toenail right off. She was repulsed, but when I told her to go get the camera, she did. She took photos, laughing through her disgust, and I saved the toenail. She still had a little fun left in her, even if I had to drag it out of her most of the time.

****

Sylvia got an apartment in Logan Square with a roommate so she could be closer to her job, and school. She'd been working her way through college ever since she'd finished high school and she was almost done with it. I'd come down and stay with her on the weekends. Eventually, I moved in. After a couple of roommates, so did Simon.

We made plans to go out West with the band and record an album; we were determined to get signed to Stinkbomb. We figured it was a long shot since The Hippie had already told us repeatedly that he wasn't interested in signing us, but his partners had quit on him a couple of years earlier so we figured we only had *one* person to con. I'd been working on tunes for two years, and they were good. No filler. I'd learned to write a bridge, and more importantly I'd learned to write to my strengths as a singer. Of course, that still meant that most of the tunes were in one of two keys, but what the hell, at least I could sing 'em. Simon was an even better bassist than The Kid and just as good a backing vocalist.

We did a short tour which ended in Oakland. The Hippie agreed to sign us to Stinkbomb Records after hearing the album during the mix sessions. The album was called *Head Attack*, and it did pretty well. Slowing down a bit and taking more time on the songwriting had paid off; both the fans and the critics loved the album and we found ourselves selling enough records that we were making a profit. No more screening our own t-shirts; we signed a deal with a company in L.A. that did all the Stinkbomb band's shirts. I quit my job and found I could just squeeze by with the bills, with a little help from Sylvia. When I could make the rent but didn't have any money left over for food, she covered me. She looked out for me. She was happy for me - happy that I didn't have to work - and I was overjoyed. I mean, finally getting one of those mythical royalty checks was a big deal.

****

Kara quit doing smack a few times but she kept going back to it. She finally went back to it after a long time of not using and must've misjudged how much she shot; she died from an overdose. Her folks didn't have much money so when her friends approached us to play a gig at the bar she used to hang out at to help pay for the funeral, we agreed. We played our set and as soon as we finished, I grabbed Sylvia and bailed out the back door, which was right behind the stage. The Duke was trying to convince me to stay: "Just one more beer old Joseph, old pal! To the memory of our good friend!" But I'd never liked bars and I didn't want to spend any time in this one. Everybody was drunk and bummed about Kara and hell, I missed the girl too but I didn't want to be around a bunch of punks all sloshed and depressed. I could've sat around drunk and told a few stories myself but it didn't feel right because her death was so wrong, so completely senseless. All I wanted was to talk to her, trade stories with her, not about her, and I couldn't do that so I decided to leave.

I'd more or less given up on Kara when she'd become a junkie and I hadn't said more than a few words to her in two years. I guess I felt a little guilty for that, but more than that, I felt that it wasn't right for her to die; she was one of the good people. I didn't go through any maybe's or what-if's; she'd been a junkie and nobody could've helped her but herself. But part of me ached because she'd wanted to live - I know that - and she, more than any of us, could have made a difference in the world. But I tried not to think about that; I would not allow myself to romanticize her death. It was stupid and pointless and entirely her fault. You live and die by choices you make and no matter how godamn smart and beautiful and full of life and wit and creativity you may be, you aren't exempt from the rules.

So many people who had been immersed in punk rock had drifted off into the military, college, straight jobs, leaving everything behind. I understood it; punk rock was a game. Even those who took it the most seriously - at least those who had spent any significant time in the scene - knew that. But it was *our* joke, a very serious joke of a lifestyle that made some strange kind of sense. There wasn't anything noble about selling off all your punk records and joining the Army, but there wasn't any more nobility in a punk rock death, your body so full of heroin that it just quits on you; shuts down for good in a bathtub while your junkie pals call 911, leave the front door open and take off with their stashes. I had to go. If I was going to get drunk and mourn, I'd do it alone.

We walked around the corner towards the car and there was Ellen sitting up against the wall next to a puddle of her own beery vomit. I remembered when Ellen had published a fanzine and played bass in a band. Once she turned twenty-one, hanging around in bars became more important. She worked at a record shop, hung out in clubs and bars and drank.

"Hey, Joe," she slurred. Her left tit was hanging out of the side of her sleeveless t-shirt. She was trying to light a joint but she couldn't get her lighter to function; she was too wasted.

"What's up?" She said.

Sylvia kept walking to the car, to warm it up. She was smart enough to keep moving past an idiot drunk. I wasn't.

"It's cold out," I said. "It's the middle of November and you're sitting here drunk in the fuckin' cold."

"What are you, my dad?"

"No," I said. "I'm sure as fuck not." I walked away. Another potential death in the making and I couldn't care. I wouldn't.

Of course, Simon brought her home an hour and a half later and they made for his bedroom - he'd finally gotten a reasonable haircut which, not surprisingly, stopped him from being a walking girl-repellent. And of course, when Ellen finally slinked out of his room around noon, she copped an attitude with me, like I'm an asshole. I'm sitting there drinking my coffee, reading the newspaper like a normal person, and she's standing there, one tit still flopping around free, dried puke on her Black Flag t-shirt, giving me a dirty look.

I was getting tired of this crap.

****

Simon was still a pothead, but when he moved in with us he became a drunk, too. We're making a little money, and of course, he's going out to the punk bars and blowing his cut of the dough. We'd get a royalty check or play a good paying gig and he'd be out buying rounds for everybody, dropping fifty, sixty bucks a night. Meanwhile, he's struggling to come up with the rent every month. And I have to be the responsible one 'cause if I'm not, everybody's broke, everybody gets jobs and everybody goes back to shooting hateful little looks at me when they think I'm not looking, like their shitty situation is my fault. We were *lucky* to be making money, didn't he get it? We were frauds but we were selling records anyway. We were still well under the poverty line but at least we didn't have to work. It was a goddamned miracle and Simon just took it for granted.

For fuck's sake, go get a job and keep it for all I care. I'd learned early on not to become too attached to anybody in the band; it was just me and Jimmy and whoever else happened to be in the band, no matter how good they were. If they had a problem, they knew they were free to leave. That's the only way it would work. If they started thinking they were irreplaceable, they would have acted ten times more stupid.

Simon had started showing signs of being a pain in the ass about two weeks after he joined the band. At first, I felt that the only real problem with him was that he was young and had never been on tour before and thus, was prone to acts of immaturity, like when we'd gone to California to record *Head Attack*. The rest of us stuck to beer; we thought pot-smoking was for hippies. But Simon was practically an addict; we had to constantly argue with him about the Band Rule concerning no illegal substances in the van. We were always getting pulled over and we didn't need to be sitting in a jail cell in the middle of nowhere because Simple Simon was always jonesing for a joint. It got to the point where we'd have to search his duffel bag before we got into the van. He finally cooled it, but only after arguing about it for about fifteen hours, like a little kid whining to stay up late.

When he realized two hours after we'd departed Rapid City that he'd left his new leather pants behind in the living room of the house where we'd stayed, he demanded that we go back to retrieve them.

"Simon, there's no way we're driving back to get those pants," I said.

"You look like a dork in those pants anyway," said Vic.

"But I just got 'em. They cost me sixty bucks!"

"Too bad. If they were so important to you, you wouldn't have left them behind in the first place." Sometimes I had to give irritating little motherly lectures to Simon. It was the only language he seemed to understand.

And Simon was a little too enthusiastic about the band; it quickly started to come off as phony. It was great to finally have a bassist who was so willing to play the way we told him to. Simon was the anti-bassist; deferential, cooperative, and always polite. On the surface, he seemed perfect. But from his first gig with us, he'd come up to the rest of us after the set and apologize for having fucked up, which was strange because he almost never made a mistake; he was by far the best musician out of all of us. "I played terrible," he'd say, as if he was really angry with himself. But he was a pretty bad actor. The first few times, we took the bait when he went fishing for compliments.

"I didn't hear you fuck up - you did great."

"No way, we've never had a bassist half as good as you."

"Dude, you're one of the best bass players in punk rock."

By the time we'd reached Oregon, we had his number. The rest of us got together and decided on the best course of action.

After our gig in Portland, the four of us were loading the gear in the van when Simon trudged over carrying his bass case.

"I'm sorry," he mumbled, eyes downcast, shuffling his feet like a bad widdle boy. "I really fucked it all up tonight. I wouldn't blame you if you found a replacement."

"Goddamn *right* you fucked up!" I yelled. "I'm getting sick of it!"

"Yeah," said Vic. "If you're gonna be in this band you can't fuck off like you've been doing every night."

"You've actually gotten *worse* since you joined the band," said Jimmy. "You're terrible!"

"I know," he answered. "I'm really sorry."

TWELVE

We had a record release party for *Head Attack* at the apartment in Logan Square. It was fun. Everybody got drunk, everybody had a good time. Well, mostly everybody. I got into it with a few of Sylvia's friends, a bunch of rich, snotty college kids who lived in Wicker Park; slumming for street credibility until they got their degrees and became respectable. But it wasn't anything too serious. Just fucking with them a little bit. Sure, one of them got pissed and left, but that always happened when I was at a party. If somebody didn't end up taking a swing at me or running around screaming "Joe Pagan is a fucking *asshole!*" it wasn't a real party.

Sylvia played the perfect hostess, smiling, making sure to talk to everybody who showed up. But after the last drunk left so did her smile.

"Why are you such a dick to my friends?"

"Because they're ninnies. Besides, I was just having fun."

"It wasn't fun for them. You made them totally uncomfortable."

"If they can't take a joke, fuck 'em."

"Who are you to judge them?"

"Who are you to judge me?"

"You know, ever since I met you, you've acted like an asshole to my friends. And you act like an asshole to me whenever anyone else is around."

"No, I only do it when you get a few beers in you and start shooting me nasty looks and making snide little comments about me. And god forbid I should start discussing anything with anybody - politics, punk rock, the weather..."

"You don't discuss, you argue. You fucking antagonize people on purpose. It's a sick little game to you."

"Maybe so, but why is it that you always side with them? You never stick up for me."

"Because you're an asshole."

"What the hell kind of answer is that?"

"You just can't help treating everybody around you like shit, can you? You're just an insecure little man."

"You're avoiding the question, which is why can't you just once stick up for me? Why do you always have to jump into the middle of a conversation that has nothing to do with you and start giving me shit? You think I'm an asshole? You oughta take a look at people's faces when you come in out of left field and start cutting me down. You always fuckin' overreact. Why is that?"

"God, why do you have to do this? Over and over like I'm being interrogated. This conversation is supposed to be about you!"

"I'm trying to *communicate* with you for fuck's sake! Why is that such a fuckin' impossibility for *you*?"

"I *can't* communicate with you because I never get to talk. You never listen, you just talk, talk, talk until I'm ready to put a gun to my head and blow my brains out to stop the sound of your voice because god knows you'll never shut up on your own. You're biologically unable to stop interrupting because everything has to be about you and how you feel and what you think. You're such a child. You can't just shut the fuck up and listen."

"I'm listening now."

"You fucking prick."

"That's what you've been waiting to tell me all these years while I did all the talking?"

She went into the bedroom and threw some clothes in a duffel bag.

"What are you doing?"

"I'd kick you out but I know you wouldn't leave so I'm going to my mom's."

"Great. This is like the fuckin' Flintstones. Go home to your mother the battle-ax."

"Fuck off."

She left, slamming the door behind her.

I called her two days later and apologized. I acted like I was apologizing for arguing with her friends, but I was really apologizing for being such a prick in general, not just the night of the party, but all the time. It seemed like it was impossible for me to communicate with Sylvia because she was such a pain in the ass, but I didn't make it any easier. I acted that way with everyone. Why try to work out a real solution or have a normal conversation when there's a smart-ass comment to be made, or when you can catch somebody in an insignificant inconsistency and hammer away at it until they're ready to kill you? Throw people off balance, frustrate them, stick it to 'em, use their own words against them and never, ever admit to them or to yourself that you're full of shit. It worked for the band, why not for real life? And what was the difference? Weren't punks supposed to be real; unpretentious? If so, that meant that I really was an asshole. But I was getting sick of it. I wasn't Joe Pagan, was I? Wasn't I Joe Peterson, just another white punk from the suburbs? Wait, who the fuck was that? I left that fucker behind in 1985, didn't I? But Joe Pagan was a character - maybe an entertaining one, but a one-dimensional, one-note, one-track mind cartoon character nonetheless. Maybe my whole life had become an act or maybe it always had been and I was just getting sick of playing the part. I knew that ninety percent of the shit that came out of my mouth was due to my own insecurities and an obsessive need to *win*. In regards to everything else, I was completely noncompetitive. I didn't give a shit if we sold more or less records than the next band. I didn't care who had a nicer apartment or who had a better car. But nobody was going to out-argue me. Sylvia was impatient, judgmental, more concerned with appearances than with substance, prone to violent tantrums and had a nasty, vindictive streak like I'd never seen in anyone else in my life. But she also loved me in spite of my idiocy and my immaturity, and she looked out for me and she was proud of me. She had a good heart in spite of the way she acted so much of the time, and

I think she must've figured that I was like her in that respect. So I apologized. And she came home and said she was sorry, too. And we fucked like a couple of coked-up monkeys.

****

Sylvia bought me a used Les Paul for my birthday - she knew I'd been wanting one and she couldn't afford a new one so she did her best, talking to my friends behind my back, trying to get a good deal. It wasn't in great shape, but it was better than my Fender copy.

I'd long ago shaved off my mohawk and stopped dyeing my hair and now I was sporting a flat top, which required a lot less care. Jimmy and I went to his barber on Belmont every other Wednesday for a touch up. I was beginning to feel respectable. We were finally selling some records and making a little money. I felt that I couldn't afford to treat tours like a vacation from a string of shitty jobs anymore; playing music *was* my job, no matter how poorly it paid.

THIRTEEN

We'd recorded a new album for Stinkbomb called *Out Of Control*, a title I hated but one that everyone else in the band and at Stinkbomb liked, and it was hard to argue with it because I'd suggested it - off the cuff maybe, but it was my idea all the same. I figured it wasn't worth starting a major argument over but I rarely missed an opportunity to let the guys in the band know that the only thing that was out of control about the record was our performances, which were under-rehearsed and sloppy. We'd been so worried about being forgotten by the crowd that had bought our previous record that we rushed to make the album even though I hadn't written more than a few good songs; most of them were written at the last minute in the studio. But in spite of its weaknesses, *Out Of Control* shot out of the gate pretty well and the rest of the band made sure to remind me of all the bitching I'd done before its release.

Sylvia decided to use her spring break from her last year in college to sell merch for us on the first leg of the tour to support the album. We started the tour in early March, and I figured it would only get warmer. I was wrong. By the time we hit Ontario, I was wishing I'd brought along my long johns. We'd bought our third van - an old Dodge beater with a creaky wooden loft in the back - for a thousand bucks and it ran fine, but the body was riddled with rusted out holes which made for a lot of long, cold, silent drives. There was always tension in the air. Don't move too close to me or I'll have to nudge you out of the way, and if you don't move, I might have to move you. Get the fuck out of the loft and let me sleep, goddamnit! Quit drooling on my pillow and gimme my half of the blanket, dick. I've been driving for seven hours and I'm tired. You go ride shotgun and try to stay alert enough to make sure we don't take the wrong highway and end up in Dayton. Arguments, bitching, reluctant apologies, always halfhearted. All part of The Tour.

At least we were finally able - barely - to afford a roadie. Al was an acquaintance from Oakland. We didn't know him real well - we'd just stayed at his house once - but I sensed that he could be trusted. Al had never worked for a band before but he was the right type; sober, alert, smart, able to think on his feet and willing to work hard. He had the roadie mindset; he actually seemed to enjoy lugging the gear out of the van and setting it up on stage. Stepping between the fists and my face. Even acting as tour manager; getting us our fair cut from sleazy and incompetent promoters; never backing down. Breaking down the gear and hauling it back to the van and then driving ten hours to the next gig. He deserved at least seventy-five bucks a day and a per diem. We could only pay him twenty plus meals.

During the drive to Toronto we had to listen to Vic's war stories about his days in the OHL.

"I ever tell you about the time I fought Jean-Guy LaCoutre?"

"Who the fuck cares?"

"Isn't he the backup goalie with the Leafs now?"

"Of course he is. What are you, retarded? This idiot has only told us this story about three hundred times."

"He was playing for London and I was with Sudbury and they were up two goals on us at the end of the third period. Two seconds left, third game of the playoffs and we're tied a game a piece right?"

"Jesus Christ, was that your biggest moment of glory?"

"Hey I played with a lot of guys who are in The Show now so shut the fuck up. I took a slapshot from Chris Pearl in the face and said good-bye to four teeth. Guy broke my fuckin' nose."

"Pearl's a drunken fuckin' bum. Keeps getting sent down to the minors 'cause he can't stop mowing down innocent Canadians in his Range Rover."

"There's no such thing..."

"Tell him that when he's aiming a shot at your throat."

"...as an innocent Canadian."

"The guy's got one of the heaviest shots in the league. Right up there with MacInnis."

"I said there's no such thing as an innocent Canadian."

"If you have to explain the joke, it's not funny, dumbbell."

"Shut up. I'm trying to tell the fuckin' story."

"Ho hum."

"Yeah, I wanna hear it."

"Oh, please proceed. This is riveting."

"So we knew we were gonna lose and we got our goalie pulled and a face off in their zone to the left of the net."

"My god, go write a book or something."

"And.. shut up... and as soon as the puck is dropped I turn around and cross check the poor frog fuck right in the chest and he *freaks*."

"You do realize that we've heard this story approximately five thousand times, right?"

"And he drops the gloves and I drop mine and before anybody can even jump in I get four big haymakers right in on his face."

"And that's why his nose is all fucked up now."

"That's right."

"Could you please, for the love of everything decent and sane tell us some other story sometime. *Any* other story!"

"You just don't get it."

"I get that you're a broken fuckin' record."

"Maybe I oughta shut your mouth."

"Maybe you oughta try. See how tough you are without a pair of ice skates on ya fuckin' pussy."

"Everybody calm down. We're almost at the show and if Joe's on a roll tonight you're gonna end up fighting the crowd instead of each other so save your energy."

"Okay. But he started it."

****

Toronto was a disaster. The promoter never showed up and the club owner had no idea what the door price was. So we charged five bucks Canadian, me and Al taking money at the door and stamping hands. Then it turned out that the stage monitors weren't working. I told the owner there was no way I was gonna play a show without monitors; my voice would be shot for the next five days.

The soundman tried to fix the monitors. He finally got them half working for the opening bands but by the time we got up to do our set, all but one of them were blown. I ended up losing most of my voice. One of the promoter's buddies approached me as we were counting the money in the back and asked me if I was happy with the way things went.

"It would have been nice if the guy promoting the show had been here," I said.

"He had a family emergency."

"Yeah," said the owner, "A family emergency at a straight edge festival in Hamilton."

"Yeah, well no wonder the show was a fuckin' train wreck."

"Well," said the promoter's pal, looking at the wad of bills on the table, "it doesn't look to me like you lost money on it. That's more than I make in a day. You oughta be grateful."

"You oughta be spanked and sent to bed without dinner."

"Fuck you!"

"Somebody get this fuckhead outta here, please. I'm losing count."

Al took him by the arm and led him out as he yelled "Sell-out" and "Rock star" at me and I got a little more tired of this so-called alternative music business that every day seemed more and more like an alternative to common sense, having one's shit slightly together and giving a crap about trying to do things in a semi-logical manner.

FOURTEEN

The gigs had gotten a little better. We were averaging five hundred a night between the door and merch. We were still sleeping on people's floors, so that kept costs down a bit.

Al was the perfect roadie. Didn't drink or use drugs, could drive a twelve hour shift without blinking an eye, willing to take a bullet for anybody in the band, always upbeat, never lost his sense of humor. Funny thing was, I was getting along better with him than I was with the other guys in the band. And Sylvia.

In the van:

"Move over!"

"I'm over as far as I can get!"

Somebody farts.

"Who did it? Goddamnit, who *did* it?"

"Not me."

"What is this, the Family Circus?"

"I don't smell anything. He who smelt it dealt it."

"That's cute. You want me to read you a bedtime story now?"

"Awww... fuck off."

"New band rule. You fart in the van without giving warning, you put a buck in the band fund."

"Bullshit!"

"Band Rule Number 118."

"Joe, stop."

"I haven't even started."

"Do you ever stop being a prick?"

"Only on Tuesdays and Saturdays."

"This sucks. I gotta piss."

"We just pulled over."

"Me too, I gotta piss."

"We're running late. Piss in the bucket."

"Fuck that."

"The piss'll smell worse than the fart."

"Fine. Al, pull over at the next gas station for the weak sister."

"Yeah, okay."

"Who farted anyway? Come on, I just wanna know."

"I didn't fart. Why's everybody looking at me? You always blame me!"

"You're a very gassy boy."

"Compared to you, I fart Chanel Number Five."

"Hey, I still gotta piss. It's starting to drip out my dick."

"Your weak bladder is gonna cost us our soundcheck."

"I don't care. It's gonna sound like shit anyway. It always does."

"I wanna get something to eat."

"We'll eat at the club."

"I think I'm gonna get a tattoo of a fork on my arm."

"What?"

"Just a fork. No explanation."

"You oughta get a tattoo of a gas gauge on your forehead pointing to 'Empty.' No explanation."

"Shut up, dick."

"How long 'til we get to the club?"

"Three days, jackass. Why don't you check your tour booklet. All the drive times are in there."

"I lost it."

"So guess."

"You're a fuckin' asshole."

"You're a fuckin' baby."

"Everybody in this band is a fucking jerk."

"Including you?"

"Shut up, I'm trying to read."

"You call 'The Little Engine That Could' reading?"

"You're a riot. When are you booked on Letterman next, funny boy?"

"Thursday. I go on right after your mother gives her horse-fucking demonstration."

"I'm warning you once, don't talk shit about my mother."

"You started it."

"And I'll end it."

"Why don't we just deal with one thing at a time?"

"Who the fuck are you, Yoko, our fuckin' manager?"

"Hey, I'm working for your band, asshole."

"Yeah, like a broken watch."

"Why do I put up with him?"

"C-U-N-T, everyone's avoiding me."

"That's a good one. That really stung."

"We're pulling over so you can piss, dumb-ass."

"I'm a dumb-ass 'cause I have to piss?"

"No, you're a dumb-ass 'cause we were just at a gas station twenty minutes ago and you didn't piss then."

"Yes I did. I just gotta go again."

"Whattya, got a leak?"

"You need some Depends?"

"Shut up."

"You shut up."

"Jesus fucking Christ, everybody just *shut the fuck up*!"

****

Sudbury didn't work out too well. My voice was still shot from the lousy monitors in Toronto and I'd made it worse by playing a full set in Sault Ste. Marie. I couldn't really sing so I tried crowd-baiting. I picked the wrong town.

By the second song in the set, I was naked.

"You got a small dick," somebody yelled.

"Your mother seemed to like it!"

"Fuck you!"

"Nice comeback dipshit. I guess I shouldn't expect anything more from a Canadian. Fuckin' donut-gobbling, hockey-watching, shitty beer-drinking douchebags."

Now the whole crowd was yelling at me. I couldn't make out the individual voices. Vic was no help. A few of his fans from when he'd been a goon defenseman had shown up as well as Chris Pearl who, despite being a virtual no-name in the NHL was pretty well known amongst the locals as an up and down fourth-liner for the Senators. Vic was practically physically distancing himself from the rest of us while Pearl was joining in on my fun, though I didn't think part of the fun should include him whipping full bottles of beer at my head. He got the joke but he didn't get the part about me not having health insurance.

"Yo, shut your pie-holes!" I yelled, dodging a bottle of Molson tossed with frightening accuracy by the Senators winger. "There's an *American* on the mic!" I continued. "Show some respect. If it wasn't for us, you'd still be eating crumpets and listening to Herman's Hermits."

Vic was turning red and appeared to be trying to hide behind his drums. Pearl was laughing hysterically and whipping beer nuts at me.

"Come down here and say that!" yelled an irate local who looked as if he'd wandered in by mistake - he had no place at a punk show. I mean, the guy had a fuckin' moustache and a mullet for chrissakes.

"Blow me, hockey head. Why don't you come up *here* and say something. Come on, I *dare* you!"

Then I started singing *America The Beautiful* and things really got out of hand. The crowd rushed the stage and we bailed out the back door. Al managed to grab the guitars and we took off in the van to a Tim Horton's a few miles down the street. Pearl showed up and shook my hand. He said, "That's the most fun I've ever had at a concert." I decided it was against my best interests to inform him that we played shows, not concerts. Besides, he was more interested in jabbering away with Vic about the good old days. There hadn't been a whole lot of Americans in the OHL in their day and they stuck together.

We waited for an hour and a half before going back to the club. The place was empty except for the owner and his staff. Amazingly, nothing had been stolen and our gear hadn't been trashed too badly. A few cracked cymbals and busted tubes, two broken drum heads. Nothing that couldn't be fixed with a quick trip to a music store. And a few hundred bucks. We'd have to eat Ramen for a few days, but we'd get on with the tour okay.

The club owner, of course, refused to pay us. He was pissed at me, but he wasn't too happy with Vic either. Told him that LaCoutre was a personal friend of his and he remembered the beating Vic had laid on the dumb French goaltender. He told us to get our shit and leave, and that he'd personally blow a hole in me with his shotgun if I ever showed my face in Sudbury again. The three bouncers by his side looked happy to accommodate him. In fact, they looked like they'd enjoy beating the shit out of me right then and there.

"Hey, what I do up on stage, it's all just part of the act," I said. "It's called crowd-baiting. It's comedy."

"I don't think it's funny," said the owner.

"That's 'cause you're Canadian," I mumbled under my breath.

"What?"

"Nothing. Thanks for the memories."

We loaded out. After we packed the van up, I noticed three garbage cans, filled to the top and standing right next to the back door.

"Hey, Al."

"What's up?" He was ready to start the van and get moving.

"Check it out." He walked over.

"What do we do?" he asked.

"Isn't it obvious?"

We dumped the trash in front of the door, made a pile about four feet high. The door swung inward. The next guy to open the door was in for a trashbath.

"Should we light it on fire?"

"I don't know," said Al. "We're not staying in town tonight, are we?"

"Nope," said Jimmy. "We have a night drive to Montreal."

"Joe," said Sylvia, "I really don't think you should do this."

"No, I'm pretty sure I should."

She was trying to be responsible and trying not to laugh at the same time. She knew it was fucked and retarded but she couldn't help seeing the humor in it, even though she was trying not to.

"I'm not bailing you out of jail."

"You won't be able to, pussycat. You'll be in there with me. So let's not get caught."

It took a couple of minutes for me and Al to get the trash heap blazing. Everyone else got in the van and Al got the motor running. I pounded my fist on the door about five times, ran like hell for the van and we took off for Montreal, laughing like crazy most of the way.

****

We stayed with some friends in Jersey City, and the house wasn't too quiet. After an all night drive, we finally got in at ten a.m., said our hellos, and promptly rolled out our sleeping bags on the living room floor and fell asleep. We were woken up by two of our host's friends after only an hour.

Sylvia demanded that we find a motel, but we couldn't afford it after getting our gear trashed in Sudbury.

"Touring sucks," I said. "I've told you that a million times. Get used to it or get on the Greyhound."

"Jesus," said Al, leaning up from his sleeping bag, "you'd make your own girlfriend take the Shame Train?"

"Why not?"

"Yeah, why not?" said Sylvia. "He's a cocksucker. He'd probably make me pay for the ticket too."

"No, I'd just take it out of your pay."

"I'm not *getting* paid."

"Well then I guess you'll have to hitch."

"Just shut your mouth, asshole."

We went out on the porch and she started yelling at me, blaming me for her inability to get a good day's sleep.

"Keep your voice down," I said.

She walked out into the street, holding up her middle finger behind her.

"Where are you going?"

"Fuck you!" she screamed.

"Yo, shut your fucking mouth, goddamnit. This is a fuckin' residential neighborhood, cunt!"

And she kept yelling and so did I, and finally, Jimmy walked out and said "Can I join in?" in that dry way of his, and I just broke up. Sylvia finally calmed down too. We all went out and found a bar that was open and got hammered. Sylvia'd had her one temper tantrum that everyone was allowed for their first tour.

"But don't push it," I told her, as I downed another beer.

****

With more money came better beer. I wouldn't even consider drinking a Budweiser anymore, not on a bet. I only drank Rolling Rock and Heineken.

l

FIFTEEN

We were home for a little under a week between gigs and me
and Sylvia got into a fight. More of a war, really, at least on my part.
For about a year, I'd had a strong gut feeling that she'd fucked around
on me at some point, long after I'd reformed. She always scoffed.

"You and your gut," she'd say. "You act like you're psychic.
You've got a G.E.D. and the job skills of a reasonably intelligent retard
but The Gut knows all."

"Hey, I might not have a high school degree," the argument
always went, "but I've followed my instincts so far and things are pretty
good."

"Yeah. You can just barely pay the rent."

"Well it doesn't matter. I know you fucked around on me. Just
admit it. It's no big deal."

She never cracked.

But this night was different. I started in on her while we were
watching TV.

"I'm telling you Sylvia, you're going to admit it someday so
you might as well get it over with now."

"You're so paranoid."

"I told you before, it's a gut feeling."

"The only thing your gut is telling you is that it wants another beer."

"Sylvia, I *know*."

And with no warning, she started crying, crying so hard she couldn't talk. She was a rock, but when she broke down, she really broke down.

"Shit, it's okay. What is it?"

"I can't..."

"Deep breaths."

It took about five minutes before she regained a little composure.

"I fucked Damon a year and a half ago."

For once I had nothing to say. I mean, I'd really known it, or at least felt it strongly, but I was still shocked. And she'd fucked my friend. Or at least I'd thought the prick was my friend.

"It was just a one-night stand," she said through sniffles. I had a strong, sudden urge to punch her in the mouth - it was the crying and the runny nose that got to me - but I ignored it.

"What the fuck."

"You cheated on me! You embarrassed me! I had to get even."

"Fuck, that was years ago. And you *got* even. I saw you blowing some jerk at a party, remember?"

"But I never *fucked* him. I never fucked him the way you fucked all those girls!"

"I'm gonna kill the fucker."

"You know he moved to Florida last year. You're not gonna drive down there to kick his ass."

"I'm losing my mind," I said. "You fucking... you're a fucking piece of shit. Go get me some beer."

"There's beer in the fridge."

"There's only two left. I counted them. One, two. Simple fucking math even for a high school drop out. Go get me some fucking beer and I swear to god if you don't come back I'm gonna drive out to your mom's and throw a molotov cocktail through her living room window 'cause I know that's where you'll be."

"I'm coming back," she sobbed, as she picked up her purse.

Ten minutes later she was back, still crying and holding a twelve pack of Rolling Rock.

I downed two beers in about two minutes, then cracked a third one and made her tell me all the details.

"Did you cum?"

"Yes."

"Great."

"Well, it wasn't that good the second time."

"The second time?"

"Yeah. We fucked twice. But his dick was so big that it started to hurt after a while."

"Oh, he had a huge dick. Thanks for the info, asshole. You think that makes me feel better?"

"I'm *sorry!*"

She told me the whole story. She'd flirted with him for a week or so, then finally gone back to the ShitHole with him, making sure to do it on a weeknight, a night when I'd be on second shift at the warehouse.

"Did you make him use a rubber?"

"Of course."

"Did you blow him?"

"A little. Just to get things started."

"Did he have a rubber on then?"

"No."

Enraged as I was, the beer was working. My head was actually more clear than it had been all night; than it had been in weeks.

"First thing tomorrow you're going for an A.I.D.S. test. That fucker has screwed more skanks than Al Capone. And I know for a fact he's got herpes."

"Okay."

"And I'm not fucking *touching* you until you get the results."

"Okay."

I cracked another beer.

"Who'd you tell?"

"I didn't tell anyone."

"Oh, come on. You're busted already. Don't insult my intelligence, okay? I know you think I'm stupid and maybe I am but I'm not *that* fucking stupid."

"I didn't tell anyone!"

"Bullshit!" I slammed the beer down on the coffee table with enough force to chip off the edge.

"The table..."

"Fuck the table."

"I'm leaving."

"Fuck you. Not this time. You fuckin' owe me, you piece of shit, and you're gonna tell me what I wanna know."

Remarkably, she stayed where she was. This was beautiful. Through all my hurt feelings and shock and humiliation, I somehow felt powerful. I was in control now and we both knew it. I really felt terrific.

Another beer.

"Who did you tell?"

She hesitated.

"I told Mary." Our old roommate.

"Who else?"

"Nobody."

"Liar, liar, pants on fire!"

"I swear I didn't tell anybody else!"

"Think a little harder."

"Okay, I guess I told Sandy."

"So you *are* a liar. Anything more to say about my gut?"

"I forgot!"

"Pen and paper."

"What?"

"*Pen and fucking paper, goddamnit!*"

"I don't know what you're talking about!" She was sobbing again. I ran into the bedroom and found what I was looking for.

"One, you fucked this dink who used to be my friend." I wrote it down.

"Yeah, but...."

"Shut up. How many times did you fuck him?"

"Twice. But it was just that one night."

"Did you fuck The Duke too?"

"God, no!"

"Was he there?"

"Well he was at the house but.."

"And he wasn't eyeing you?"

"Look, he wanted to fuck me, I could tell, but I wasn't interested in him. He was jealous. He thought he'd get sloppy seconds but I left."

"Where'd you go?"

"I came home."

Another beer.

"Who else did you tell?"

"I already told you, nobody."

"Yeah, you told me that before. Who the fuck else did you tell?"

One by one, reluctantly, she divulged the names. I wrote them all down. Five of her friends, each time saying she'd forgotten about telling them until just now.

Another beer, pounding them down as fast as I could. I had a list of who she'd told. I'd written down all the details she'd told me. I went over it five, six, seven times with her. I told her to call one of the friends she'd told. She made the call to Sandy.

"I'm gonna hand the phone to Joe," she said. "Tell him exactly what I told you about me and Damon last year."

The story was essentially the same one she'd told me. I hung up without saying good-bye.

"You sucked his dick, you fucked him twice, and then you got dressed, drank a beer and left without fucking The Duke."

"Yes."

"And you only told these five friends." I recited their names.

"Yes."

Another beer.

"I think you're still lying."

"I'm not. And I'm so sorry. I did it to get back at you but I never wanted to tell you because I didn't want to hurt you."

"What's the point in getting back at somebody if they never even know it?"

"I..."

"Shut the fuck up. You're fucking demented, you know that? Yeah, I was a sleazebag but I never nailed one of *your* friends. And I was fucking wracked with guilt. Why do you think I ended up telling you? I couldn't sleep right 'cause I felt guilty. Did you?"

"No," she admitted.

"Do you now?"

"I feel bad for making you feel bad."

"You're fucked. You're getting that A.I.D.S. test, and you're gonna get tested for syphilis and herpes and any other goddamn thing that fucker gave you and when I go back out on tour I've got carte blanche, pussycat. I'm fucking anything I want to, and you're gonna keep your legs crossed and your mouth shut and if you don't like it then you can get the fuck out of here right now."

"Okay," she said. "Okay."

She went to bed.

Another beer. I slept on the couch. By the time Simon got home, the storm had passed. I still felt sick about the whole thing, but I kinda felt like laughing too. After all, I'd been right all along.

SIXTEEN

The second leg of the tour was all down south and out west. We went over the rules on the drive down to Nashville.

"No promotion for the show, we bail, no matter how many people are there, right? Band Rule Number 206."

Everybody agreed.

"No stage monitors, we bail, no matter how many people are there. Band Rule Number 207."

No disagreements.

"Somebody stands with the counter at the door and counts the people who pay to get in, right? Band Rule Number 208."

The rules were set. Everyone was on the same page. Jimmy was running out of room to write the band rules on the inside of the roof of the van with his marker. But we all liked laying in the loft looking up at the rules we knew we'd all broken and that we'd continue to break, willfully and with a committed regularity.

****

We stayed with Bill and Tina down in Lake Havasu. We barbecued some chicken and ribs in their back yard before the show, and one of Bill's pals gave me a couple of passes to the nudist resort where he worked. Vic and I decided to go there after the gig. Tina had a little poodle that was running around yipping at everybody but it seemed to particularly dislike Simon. Bill finally had to lock the pooch in the bedroom so Simon wouldn't get bitten.

When we got to the club, the promoter loaded us up with drink tickets. I grabbed a couple of pitchers of beer and headed over to a cute blonde sitting at a table by herself. I sat down across from her and refilled her glass.

She told me she was going to school in Tempe. She didn't know anything about punk rock; she'd just seen a flier on campus and thought she'd check out the show 'cause the band had an interesting name and she was going to be in town to visit her folks anyway. I talked to her for a little while before telling her I was in the band. She didn't seem too impressed. "What's the name mean?" she asked.

"Oh, it's a statement about uh... well, it's all about religion and the sham of the American Dream and all that." I didn't have the balls to tell her we'd swiped it from the title of a Saccharine Trust record because it sounded cool.

Bill's band, The Killer Meteors, opened up. They threw lit cigarettes and smoke bombs into the crowd. Bill started swinging the mic around by the cord during their third song and ended up hitting some kid in the front row. Fucked his nose all up. Later on in the set, a skinhead was causing trouble out in the crowd, throwing people around. Bill told him, "Cut it out or I'm gonna come down there, put a dress on you, and fuck you." That stopped the big prick in his tracks.

There was no ventilation in the club. No air conditioning, no fans, nothing. It must've been over a hundred degrees inside. Fifteen minutes into our set I was close to keeling over. I was seeing double, feeling the beer in my gut swirling around all hot and pukey. I was about to fall over on my head when some skins started beating on a punk. The punk's girlfriend freaked and sprayed Mace all over the place. Everybody bailed out of the club. I went out to the parking lot and took a few hundred deep breaths. Then I found the Mace girl and gave her a few pieces of my mind.

"I didn't wanna see your shitty sell-out band anyway!" she screamed.

"Oh yeah?" I yelled back. "You just paid five bucks to see my shitty band, you dumb cunt!"

I found College Girl and asked her if she wanted to go to the nudist resort with me.

"Do they have rubbers there?" she asked.

"I'm sure they do," I said. "I'm sure they do."

By the time we got to the gate, it was raining a little so the security guard wouldn't let us in. We drove back to Bill's place, but by then she wasn't in the mood. We got out of her little red sportscar and I tried kissing her, but she was having none of it. We went in the house and laid down next to the guys on the floor. I was too horny to sleep and College Girl was either too sleepy or too bored with me to fuck.

When I woke up, College Girl was gone. I looked over at Simon, laying on his side, mouth wide open, drooling. There was something right next to his mouth. I stood up to get a better look. It was a pile of dog shit. I looked around for the poodle. She was sitting in the kitchen. I swear, that dog was smiling. I woke up the other guys as quietly as possible so we could have a little photo session.

"That's gonna make a great record cover," said Vic.

****

We played San Diego and a local promoter who'd ripped us off years ago showed up. I was just hanging out in the club - there was no backstage area - and I see this big, fat jerk milling around.

"Hey fuckhead," I said as I approached him. "You still owe us two hundred bucks."

"I don't owe you anything."

"Motherfucker, what do you have in your wallet right now?"

"Fuck you!"

"How'd you like it if I kicked your ass right here?"

"Go ahead and try, pussy."

I started taking my jacket off.

"After I beat the shit out of you I'm gonna drag your fat ass to the nearest ATM."

"We'll see, tough guy."

Before my jacket was even off the bouncers had stepped in and that was that. I didn't want to throw the first punch anyway. I never had before and I didn't really wanna start now.

"What's the matter with you?" said Jimmy. "I've known you all my life and I've never seen you start a fight."

"I don't know. I'm just fuckin' pissed off, that's all. The guy screws us then shows up at one of our gigs. It's not right."

"True, but there's no point in breaking your hand on the guy's face. You still won't get our money and you'll probably end up in jail."

"I know. It's over. I acted like an idiot. Forget it."

We played our set and everything went fine. But I was pissed, and not over some jackass who'd ripped us off. I hated what punk rock had become, or maybe I was just seeing it in a different light. People came out to the shows like automatons; puppets who moved according to the way they thought they were supposed to. Most of the bands tended to be bored as well; at least in that it was a mutual relationship. But we received money for propping our corpses up on the stage. The lemmings in the crowd didn't even have the promise of a little excitement between the time they jumped off the cliff and smashed to pieces on the ground. It was a way to fill the time, to be done as quietly and with as little movement, eye contact or emotion as possible.

On the rare occasions when they were somewhat animated, the crowd was invariably, monumentally, aggressively stupid. Yelling out song titles like they were watching a wedding band. Screaming "Fuck you" - there's one of those at every show - over and over and over for thirty, forty minutes straight. Shoving each other around and beating each other up; getting shoved around and beaten up and doing nothing about it, and don't make the mistake of counting on anybody else in the crowd to lend a hand. We were their ersatz television; their baby-sitter for the night. And when it came right down to it, the pay wasn't really enough. Maybe I was just getting old, but it seemed like things were starting to change for the worse.

After our set Al got our money and loaded out the gear. I went out to the van with Vic and Simon. Al was leaning up against the side of the van waiting for Jimmy, who was still inside doing the merch count with the club manager. I was sitting in the driver's seat, Vic was in the shotgun seat and Simon was in the back. Some brain dead mohicaned guy who'd been hanging around talking to Al and Simon all night walked out with three other punk rockers. They were drunk. They walked to the front of the van, and the Punk yelled at me, "Hey rock star! Gimme a t-shirt."

This was not new territory for me. I was actually very well-equipped to deal with such a situation. I did what I always do; what usually helped me avoid violence. I rolled up the window, locked the door, avoided eye contact and said, loud enough for him to hear, "No." His friends, meanwhile, immediately got a "we know what's coming" look on their faces and left. Turned on their heels and walked away, never to return. We would've just driven off, but we were still waiting on Jimmy.

"Come on," he said. "You have money. You write for *Punk Bible*." I had no idea why he thought I got a salary for writing a column for a stupid fanzine. That goddamned column I'd been writing for years - with the sole intention of pissing people off - had helped bring some attention to the band, but unfortunately it was primarily negative. I got more hate mail than the other columnists, and more death threats - and that was good for hyping up the band - but I also got jerks like this showing up at gigs wanting to knock an imaginary chip off my shoulder, or maybe just wanting to be able to say they took a swing at Joe Pagan.

I could tell Simon was getting nervous - he hated confrontations. He said, "I don't know what's wrong with that guy. Ten minutes ago he was offering to put us up and cook us dinner."

I ignored Simon and told the Punk "No," again, still not making eye contact. This went on for a while as he circled the van. Finally, he walked over to my side of the van and opened a bottle of Bud. He said that he didn't mean anything by calling me a motherfucker, a rock star and a sell out. He asked me to please roll the window down so he could just talk to me. I said "No" in the same way that I had numerous times already. He repeated his request several times. When he realized I wasn't going to roll the window down, he started calling me an asshole again. Al approached him and told him that I was having a shitty day and that maybe he should just leave.

"I just want to talk to him."

"Why don't you back off. Come on."

He ignored Al and turned back to me.

"Roll down the window."

"No."

So he screamed, "Fuck you!" and smashed his full bottle of beer against the driver's side window, which was conveniently located about three inches from my head.

These things always happen fast, really fucking fast; no time to think. You act or you don't. In the time it took to try to figure out whether the window had broken through, we were already moving, all except Simon, who stayed in the backseat. By the time I was out the door, Al had the Punk by the front of his t-shirt and had already hit him in the face a few times. Me and Vic started hitting him too; I popped him about fifteen times in the kidneys. He covered up and hit the ground as Vic was kicking him in the stomach. He curled up in a fetal position, and for reasons of which I'm still not entirely sure, we all stopped at the same time. His eyes were closed and he wasn't moving or making a sound; he'd made no attempt to fight back. I had no idea how severely we'd beaten him. I leaned down and made sure he was breathing. I said, "He's not dead, anyway." Jimmy walked out and we took off.

During the ride up to L.A. I was happy to learn that Al had the same sick feeling in his stomach that I did. Vic disagreed: "The motherfucker *fucked* with us. We *had* to kick his ass!" But we weren't fighters; the guy had it coming but I couldn't get any joy out of beating the shit out of him. I was disgusted, and eager to get the fuck away from San Diego. As far as I was concerned, this wasn't a good sign of things to come.

****

We played L.A. the next night. During the opening bands' sets, I sat backstage with Jimmy and the owners of the club, watching the Dodgers-Braves game. When we came out to do our set, the place was already pulsating. We had a good crowd. Energetic, primed, ready to have fun. The kind of crowd you didn't see much anymore.

About halfway through the set, some kid up front started spitting on me. I kept shaking my head at him while trying to sing and play guitar. He kept spitting. When the song ended, I threw my guitar behind me and jumped off the stage. I grabbed him by the front of his shirt and swung him around.

"No, no no!" he said. "I was just fucking around, man. I'm sorry!" I let him go and the bouncers took him outside. Just another dumb kid who'd seen too many punk rock movies.

When we finished the set, I saw Al holding a bloody washcloth to his forehead. The idiot that I am, I'd thrown my guitar off, not thinking it might land on the guy who was working the stage for us. He had a huge gash above his right eye, courtesy of one of the tuners on the head of my guitar. Between that and the bruised knuckles from the night before I'm surprised he didn't ask me to set up a worker's comp. program.

Luckily, there was a paramedic-in-training at the show. He came out to some of the local shows to practice his craft should anyone get hurt. It was sheer, blind luck; there's usually nothing resembling a medical person within miles of any punk show. He told Al he could either go to the County Hospital - none of us had health insurance - where he'd wait for at least twelve hours before getting stitched up, or the paramedic could fix him up in the parking lot - but there would be a scar. There was no question.

After the paramedic fixed Al's head, he tended to the kid who had been spitting on me. The kid had taken a couple of hits of acid before the show and was now laying in the parking lot, smashing his fists against the pebbles on the ground, screaming *"Jesus!"* over and over. The paramedic and the promoter took him backstage and tried to get him to come down.

"Count to ten."

"One, two... three... *jesus blood god jesus jesus fuck christ jesus!*"

"Whoa, slow down, you're okay. Start again at one."

I felt awful. I always ended up feeling awful for the guys who fucked with me.

The next night we played Bakersfield. We went and ate with the promoter at a Subway across from the club. He pointed out a greasy, longhaired guy who was sitting on the sidewalk in front of the club.

"That guy always bugs me to let him work security, but I had to tell him no tonight," he said. "He doesn't do much of anything anyway. He's just a coke addict. But he's been giving me a hard time."

Naturally, just as we were about to do our set, the guy cornered me backstage.

"They wouldn't let me work security," he said. "So I had to pay five bucks. I'm fuckin' broke."

"That's too bad," I answered, wondering why he was telling this to me.

"They said I could have my five bucks back if somebody starts trouble and I help out."

"Yeah?"

"Yeah, so do me a favor and start some shit."

I assumed he was kidding, and I kind of laughed.

"No, really. You're an asshole, I've heard the stories."

"What? You're insane. No! Go away."

"Come on man, what the fuck. I heard about that guy you beat up in L.A. last night."

"Look," I said. "I didn't beat up anybody last night. You've got your facts wrong, pal. I'm not going to do anything, and *you're* not going to do anything."

He told me to fuck off and walked away.

I kept my eye on him throughout the whole set. I made a point of trying to dispel the rumors of our violence when we took the stage but some jerk shouted out that he'd been at the L.A. show and had seen me beat up a guy in the crowd. That didn't help matters but the night was ruined anyway. The crowd was treated to a tentative, tight-assed set from four guys who were all watching one stupid fucking coke head like a bunch of worried old women.

SEVENTEEN

The Fresno gig was a bust - no P.A., no promoter in sight, not a flier in town - but some of the guys had friends that were supposed to show up. I reminded them that we'd agreed to bail out on any fucked-up shows. They got back in the van reluctantly and we headed up to Oakland. On the way up, me and Jimmy got into a fight about it.

"I was supposed to meet that girl from Bakersfield at the gig," he said. "I don't even have her number."

"Well, I'm sorry but the show was fucked and we all agreed to bail out on any shows that were fucked. Band Rule Number 206. Or 207. I forget."

"But what's wrong with one exception on the whole tour?"

"Because, you know, one turns into two, into three, and the whole tour ends up being a circus."

"Well," said Simon, wiping the lenses of his glasses over and over with the bottom of his t-shirt, "I don't know what the big deal is. We all had friends showing up at the gig. Everybody but you." Wipe, wipe, wipe.

"Man, you've been stoned and drunk for a solid week. Who the fuck are you to say anything? You seem to think you can't be replaced. If Jimmy wants to argue with me, fine, but you haven't earned the right."

"I've been in this band long enough to have a say." He continued to clean his glasses like an obsessive-compulsive beaver gathering twigs for a dam. It was driving me nuts.

"Pal, you're deluded. Me and Jimmy started the band and we'll end it. If you don't like it, you can both beat it. I'll replace you so fast your head'll spin."

"Why don't you lay off him," said Vic.

"Why don't you butt out?"

"Whatever," he said, climbing up into the loft. "Wake me up when the cat fight's over."

Everybody was quiet for a while. Then Simon finally put his glasses on and spoke up again.

"I've been thinking about getting my own place after the tour."

"That's good," I snapped back. "Me and Sylvia decided to kick you out a month ago and I've just been waiting for the right time to tell you."

It was the truth - he never paid the rent or bills on time - but I didn't need to say it. I don't know why I always had to do that. I liked Simon okay but he bugged the hell out of me sometimes and my knee-jerk reaction was always to use a sledgehammer to kill a gnat instead of dealing with it rationally. The van was silent for the rest of the ride and I felt like an asshole, and then I felt pissed off about feeling like an asshole because it was *those* guys that had started pissing and moaning. But I still shouldn't have said that to Simon. The idea that you can be right and still be a prick never entered my head.

****

After making some decent money at our Bay Area shows, we travelled back across I-80 playing shitty gigs with low attendance and arguing with promoters about our cut of the door money. After we'd refused to give an extra twenty bucks to one of the opening bands in Salt Lake City, we walked outside to find all the tires slashed on the van. We missed the next gig and had to shell out almost five hundred bucks to replace the tires. By the time we got to Minneapolis we were exhausted. We stayed at a college kids' house - the promoter had set it up. We'd driven all night and I slept for a few hours on a cot in the foyer before going upstairs to shower. I saw a girl sitting on her bed in one of the rooms, reading. I walked over to the doorway.

"Thanks for letting us stay here," I said.

"It's no problem. We put up all the bands that come through." I noticed that she had a few Henry Miller books on her shelves.

"I like some of Miller's stuff okay, I guess," I said. "But I've been trying to read *Tropic Of Capricorn* for two years, which either means he's boring or I'm a moron."

"You're a moron," she said. "Maybe you can handle this." She handed me a copy of *The Lover*.

I figured it would spoil the moment to tell her I'd read it years ago and hated it. I closed the door and sat down on the edge of the bed. She laid down and pulled up her shirt. Her tits were huge, and she had large, dark nipples that almost covered her breasts. I love those kind of nipples. Too many preteen years spent poring over photos of African women in *National Geographic*, I guess.

"I like big tits," I noted, ever the witty conversationalist. I didn't care about tits. I always told girls I liked their tits, no matter what the size. They're always so worried about them. That and their asses. You never hear a girl complaining about her pussy.

"My boobs used to bother me," she said. "But I finally decided that anybody who doesn't like them can go fuck themselves."

"I'm with you. I like 'em."

We undressed and fucked. I got off in about two minutes and went and took a shower.

****

Whenever I came home from a tour, Sylvia would run a bath for me and let me lay there in the tub with a cold beer while she washed me. Then she'd stand me up, dry me off and bring me into the bedroom or the living room and the next thing I know, I'm fucking her doggy style, my dick slamming in and out of her. This time was no different. As soon as she got home from work she gave me the post-tour workout. After we were done we both slumped on the couch, naked. She asked me if I'd fucked anybody on tour.

"It doesn't matter," I said. "It's over. I forgive you. Why do you wanna know, anyway?"

"I don't know. I just..."

"You get the A.I.D.S. test?"

"Yeah. Negative."

"Fine, then it's over."

"I just..."

"Just forget it. The tour sucked and I'm glad to be home."

She wasn't satisfied with that but I guess she still felt bad enough to leave it alone.

EIGHTEEN

I'd grown to hate touring. The same rip-off promoters, the same crowds in every town, same faces; some blank, some hopeful, some excited, some angry, but always the same people who looked and behaved exactly like the people we'd played to in a different town the night before; and now there were autograph seekers and hangers-on to contend with, too. It had turned into a job and I hated it almost as much as I'd hated any other job I'd ever had. But I inevitably ended up bored when I was home.

A few days after the tour, Sylvia and I went out to see a movie in Des Plaines. I don't know why we went to Des Plaines - it was the dollar theater out in the suburbs; I'd started making enough money to afford a first run movie in a theater closer to home. And I don't know why I even bothered to get Sylvia to call in sick to work. She hated doing it; she felt some weird sense of responsibility. I hated her attitude towards work. If I'd been making enough money, I would've asked her to quit her job. I don't think she would've. She was the kind of girl who would win the lottery and keep working, just out of boredom. Whatever hopes and dreams she might've once had were blocked out, the same way she'd always blocked out anything that made her give consideration to any thought or feeling that approached the realm of emotional reality. She was depressed, but I was too self-obsessed to notice it. And when I finally did notice it, I quickly realized there wasn't anything I could do about it. We just couldn't seem to talk no matter how many words were spoken; the words didn't mean anything to either one of us - just senseless babble that invariably turned into an argument.

I don't remember the name of the movie. Some unbearable piece of shit, I remember that. Probably starring Michelle Pfeiffer or Juliette Lewis; one of those bony, talentless, hideous she-things that passes for beauty with the nine to five set. Sylvia liked those sappy romantic comedies. I hated them. But I went, I guess, because I was bored, and sitting around in a movie theater with her at 12:30 in the afternoon reasonably drunk on six or seven Heinekens seemed like it would be more fun than sitting around the apartment alone at 12:30 in the afternoon watching talk shows and cartoons totally drunk on nine or ten Heinekens.

Naturally the theater was almost empty, it being the first show of the day. We sat near the middle of the theater, on the aisle.

I put my feet up and opened a beer. And I started in on the movie, making cracks every time something stupid was said or done, which was fairly constantly.

"Shut up," said Sylvia.

"I can't help it," I said. "I paid to see a movie. The movie sucks. I certainly have the right to say so." It wasn't like I'd been yelling. Just making a few quiet comments here and there. Well, and occasionally yelling "Oh my *god!*" whenever Julia Roberts or Darryl Hannah or whoever the hell it was would show her deformed, crablike face on the screen.

"Well, I like the movie, so why don't you just shut the fuck up."

"How can you like this shit?" I asked. "This movie encompass..." I couldn't remember how to pronounce the word. "It fucking *embodies*," I started again, "every goddamn thing wrong with this society."

"It's just a movie. Why don't you have another beer, you drunk."

"I haven't finished this one yet, dear."

"You smell like you've finished the brewery."

"Where do they brew this stuff anyway? Holland?"

"*Shut up!*"

"I was just wondering, is it German? Sounds like German to me: *Heine-ken*. Probably means 'of the asses of the bovines of Deutschland.' You should know, my evil little kraut princess."

"Why do you always do this?"

"Do what? I'm merely trying to ascertain the origin of the beer." I pulled that one off nicely. Even pronounced "ascertain" and "origin" correctly. Quick, clean, the way I liked it.

"Look at the fucking label if you want to know where the beer came from and please shut your big fucking mouth so I can watch the movie."

"Well, okay then."

I was almost asleep when the light flashed in my face.

"Sir, please take your feet off the seat."

"What? What? Who are you? What is this?" I knew, of course, who it was - it was the usher. Hell, I'd worked in a movie theater.

"Sir, please take your feet down."

"Okay. Get your flashlight out of my face." He waited - a nineteen year-old kid with an attitude - until my feet were down before he removed the light.

Awake and cranky, I asked Sylvia for a blowjob.

"No. I'm watching the movie."

"How about a handjob?"

"Joe, *fuck off.*"

So I put my feet back up and really *did* fall asleep.

Then the light woke me up again, along with its owner's insistence that my feet come down.

"My fiancee," I said loudly, "is trying to watch the movie. Stop making so much goddamn noise." Sylvia sighed aggressively.

"Sir, I've already asked you once."

"Okay," I said, getting to my feet. I stumbled and had to grab the seat in front of me to keep from falling on my face. It wasn't the alcohol; all the blood had rushed from my feet and I couldn't stand properly. Sylvia made disgusted noises deep in her throat.

"Let's" I gasped, "talk about this in the lobby." I concentrated on my mission and began hobbling up the aisle behind my tormentor.

Once we were in the lobby it took a few seconds for my eyes to adjust to the light.

"Now look, junior," I said, squinting. "I was just having a little nap, that's all. Why did you have to harass me?"

"Sir," he began. I cut him off.

"Call me 'sir' one more time and I'm going to spank you." I wasn't much bigger than him but I was sure I *looked* terrible. He looked like he wanted to back away but he stayed where he was.

"I've asked you twice to keep your feet off the seats."

"Yes, you have, which begs the question: *Why?*"

"So that the other people who paid to *see* the movie can see it. They can't see it if your feet are in the way."

"What if," I began, "I were freakishly tall and had an enormous head..." then I stopped myself. "Wait a minute. There's nobody behind us. Not a soul."

"That's not the point."

"No. Wrong. That's *exactly* the point. You just said so. Now you're contradicting yourself. You're completely out of control. You've become a power freak. You're fucking *dangerous*, people like you."

He'd become visibly nervous. I moved in closer to him. He stood his ground, barely.

"It's the theater's policy that nobody is allowed to put their feet up on the seats in front of them," he managed to croak.

"What about the seats behind them? Never mind, that was stupid." I tried to think clearly. It was obvious I was dealing with a lunatic. This was no time to let the Heineken do the talking.

"So what you're telling me," I said loudly, "is that even in a nearly empty theater, with not a single human in our vicinity, is that your obsession with the placement of my feet comes down to *rules*?"

Nobody likes being called a stick in the mud. But he had a job to do and he took it seriously.

"Those are the rules, sir and..."

"*Don't* fucking call me *sir*. Jesus Christ, I already told you."

"And I told you to put your feet down." The little fucker was getting *bold* with me.

"Listen, I used to work at a movie theater, too. And thank god I didn't take it as seriously as you take your three dollars and thirty-five cents an hour job, sport, because if I did I never would have had the balls to quit that job and go on to make a living playing rock and roll, a nice living which has resulted in my being able to take in this afternoon's abomination free of thoughts of work or any other responsibilities." I'd actually been fired from that job but there was no need to tell him that. Besides, I'd been about to quit anyway.

"I'm just telling you the rules are..."

"I don't care. Leave me alone. I'm going back to my seat now. My wife is probably worried to death. She probably thinks you've had me arrested for wreaking havoc on your theater seats."

"You said she was your fiancee just a few minutes ago."

"We're getting married this afternoon."

"Just keep your feet down." He made no attempt at being pleasant about it.

"For no other reason than those are the rules."

"Yes, and they're there for a good reason."

"Fine, Mussolini. Where were you when the Spanish Inquisition needed you?" With that I turned and made my way back to the theater.

When I got back to my seat, Sylvia didn't say a word.

"How's the movie?"

"You ruined it." Then, a little less cold, "It sucks anyway."

"How about a blowjob?"

"No way. You're drunk. You'll take forever to cum."

"Come on, pussycat. I'm really horny. I'll cum quick."

"When we get home."

"I'll cum in two minutes. If I don't, I'll wait 'til we get home."

I unbuttoned my pants and pulled my already hard dick out through the flap in my boxers.

"Two minutes," she said. "I'm counting." But I could tell she liked this. She loved the idea of sex in public. She was always bugging me to drive to make-out spots to fuck, maybe catch other people fucking. And since I knew it turned her on and I really *was* ready to bust, I beat that two minute deadline with a good thirty seconds to spare.

And it just so happened that at the very moment my balls decided to contract and shoot out the fruit of Sylvia's labor, the flashlight shined in my face. At first, the usher didn't quite understand what was going on. The female manager he had brought with him didn't understand either. I only saw a glimpse of her; she was actually very good looking, about my age, full pouty lips, big tits. Then, as if it had a mind of its own, the flashlight swung down to my crotch.

This all happened so quickly that Sylvia didn't have much time to react. She chose the wrong moment. As she pulled away, I came all over the side of her face. The manager started shrieking, then gagging. She ran up the aisle making awful choking sounds, her faithful lap dog close behind.

"We should leave," I said. I fished around in my jacket pocket for some Kleenex and handed it to Sylvia. She did the best she could in the near dark. We hustled out to the lobby but Sylvia insisted on going to the bathroom to wash her face. I elected to wait in the car.

When she came out, she said, "You'll never believe what happened."

"Tell me."

"That woman, she was in the bathroom *puking*."

"No way!"

"Yes! It was hilarious! She was in the stall so she couldn't see me. I didn't bother cleaning up my face. I just said, 'Come on honey, you've never seen cum before?' and then I got out of there."

We laughed about it most of the way home, but by the time we were back at the apartment she was pissed off.

"I can't believe I missed a day of work for that."

"It was fun. It's a story to tell. Only when we tell it, we should say that she puked right there in the theater."

"We're not telling this story. *You're* not telling this story. Ever!"

See, the problem was, she was growing up. And I was just sort of hanging around, waiting for something new to happen. I'd always known it would happen; that she'd outgrow me, become an adult. I knew then we weren't going to last.

NINETEEN

Simon moved out right after the tour and a few weeks later we recorded our fifth album, *Manifesto For The Aggressively Stupid*. I took complete control of the album. I'd always run things within the band creatively, but I became kind of a maniac about this album. I knew without question the way it was supposed to sound, how it should be sequenced, what the title should be, what the art should look like, and anybody who dared suggest otherwise got an earful. The engineer did a couple of mixes that didn't satisfy me. I called Stinkbomb and asked The Hippie to book mixing time with the guy who'd recorded us in California two years earlier. A week later, I flew into San Francisco and rented a car. I'd be there for four days, staying at Al's in Oakland.

I was only twenty-five but I felt old. And stupid. The band was doing well considering we weren't technically very good. I'd reached the point where I could write a decent tune fairly consistently and we'd gotten better but we were still weak musicians at best. Every time we finished an album I felt like I'd just pulled myself back up to the ledge of the cliff by my fingernails. I felt like a con artist, not a recording artist. Worse, I wasn't saving any money. I was making the rent and then some, but I just bought things when I had extra cash, or lent people money, never bothering to get it back. My folks were barely able to pay the rent on their house in Round Lake but my old man refused to borrow money from me. I'd visit them and slip a few hundred bucks to my mother when the old man was out of the room. She always paid me back even though I told her not to. My friends never paid me back.

I knew I should be thinking about the future but I'd never liked to do that; I couldn't see anything ahead of me except dragging my stupid, drunken ass around the country for the next twenty years. Getting legitimized by the mainstream press ten years after I'd done anything relevant. Playing the old hits for fans too young to have seen the real thing the first time around. The record was great but the record was now and I was never able to sit down and appreciate now.

I kept thinking of Wayne Newton with a mohawk. What would it be like to be singing punk rock songs to toothless old geezers with oddly-placed earrings and butchered and dyed hair, still trying to fuck the cutest old hags in the crowd? Being a musician - and I only called myself that on my tax forms - was about the dumbest occupation a person could have. I hated musicians. Pretentious, spoiled, rock star crybabies. But I really didn't have any other choice.

During the day I drove up to the studio in the North Bay with The Hippie and worked. The Hippie must've sensed my maniacal need for control; for once he actually kept his big mouth shut. The Hippie *always* had an opinion. The Hippie *always* had some disparaging remark to make; build you up one minute by telling you you were the greatest band since the Ramones, then tear you down the next by suggesting your new album wasn't worth the vinyl it was pressed on. But this time, he kept quiet, maybe sulking a little. He sat around eating Oreos and potato chips; wheezing and groaning as he attempted to practice yoga; chain-smoking clove cigarettes and pot; reading the newspaper while I redid vocal takes, added guitar overdubs and a few weird samples just to fuck with the punks. If The Hippie started being a pain, I'd walk out front and yell back to him that I'd seen a stray cat in the parking lot. That always got rid of him for an hour or so.

The studio was in an industrial park. Not much to see except a deli where I could get a decent sandwich before 6:00. But on the second day, I saw some big muscleheads heading into a garage. I walked over and looked inside. They had a ring set up and they were wrestling. Not collegiate wrestling, but *wrasslin'*. Irish Whips, Springboard Planchas, chairs to the back of the head, all that stuff. The next night when we were leaving the studio, I asked the Hippie if he'd mind if we hung around for a minute to watch; they were filming a match outside. The Hippie placated me, barely amused by the goings on but probably too tired to argue.

Two guys were throwing each other up against the side of the building, doing leg drops off cars, belly-to-belly suplexes onto the ground, smacking each other around with two-by-fours. The bigger guy snapped off a car antenna and whipped the smaller guy across the head with it. The crowd - all of thirty people - was going nuts. The big guy was the heel, naturally, and his valet - one of those hideous, overly made-up heavy metal girls - was running around, tits bouncing, almost-bare ass jiggling while she tried to help her man by tripping up his opponent. She had just punched the little guy in the balls when a car came driving into the lot, slowly. The babyface recovered from his testicular misfortune in time to throw the goon in front of the car. The heel hit it and sold it, flying onto the hood and apparently trying to smash the windshield in with his head.

We drove back down to the city and I couldn't stop thinking how much it was like punk rock. Abusing yourself; doing mindless, pointless, useless shit for a tiny crowd that would turn on you the second you made something better of yourself. Entertaining the drunken fools for whom TV had gotten boring, but for whom reality was still too frightening to face. Create a new reality: This is ours and it's real and we live the *life*, motherfucker. Never knowing for a second how idiotic they looked. You don't perform Shakespeare for zoo animals, do you? Keep one small step ahead of them, which - if you have any brains at all - takes only the slightest effort, and they clap their hands with glee; salivate as you stand in front of them in all your geek glory; scream as you bring shameless self-promotion and nauseatingly false humility to new highs. Turning something you know is fake into something real, even as you proclaim its inherent bogosity. Musicians and wrestlers. If it weren't for actors, we'd be the scum of the entertainment world.

The funny thing was, all my friends, hell, even my girlfriend, were people who I'd met through punk rock. I'd slept on strangers' floors and strangers had slept on mine; there'd never been any question of anybody stealing your stuff. Nobody had much of anything to steal anyway. We were a bunch of fiercely individualistic, wired, crazy motherfuckers who couldn't even stand each other's company long enough to create anything cohesive. It just kept turning: A new band, an old band, a new kid, an old guy. Middle-aged punk at twenty-five. A turnover that would make your average McDonald's franchise look stable but there was never a lack of bodies to take the place of those who bailed; bitter, frightened, or just maybe a little too smart to stick around watching the same old re-runs night after night. Nah, fuck 'em. We were the smart ones. The ones who moved on - they were fucked. Whoever said that misery loves company must've been a punk rocker.

The wheel kept on turning. It creaked like a motherfucker, but it turned. Nobody worried about anybody stealing their stuff. Like I said, there was nothing to steal.

SUCKER

TWENTY

Y'know how you *know* you're fucked when you've got half a second to think before the idiot in the Camaro smashes into the side of your car? You tense up for it. You convince yourself you're ready. And you never are. I saw it coming. Headed right for me, brakes out, no time to sort it out, no time to move. But I couldn't stop it and I figured I'd just brace myself; clench my teeth, tighten my grip on the wheel, try to stop my head from jerking forward and smashing through the windshield and I might make it through okay. Get a good lawyer and I just might make a few bucks off it.

I wasn't the only one. Most of my friends were just as dumb as me. When punk hit it big, we thought we'd broken in. The fat cats, the in-crowd, the scenemakers, they didn't know what they were doing when they invited us to the big party in their mansion. Eat as much food as you can, drink all their beer, steal anything that isn't nailed down and get the fuck out before they figure out that you don't really belong. Christ, like a bad movie. Did we really believe they were that dumb? How could we forget everything we'd learned; everything we'd always known? Things were suddenly going to change from the way they'd always been from the beginning of time because we were smarter? What arrogance. *We* were gonna play *them*? And, of course, that's how we got played. Walked right in swinging around our big balls, practically begging for 'em to be cut off. Was there ever a bigger group of chumps than the punks who thought they could play ball with the big boys and win? Grade-A suckers, that's what we were. There was no excuse. We got what we deserved.

****

There were three bands who hit it big by signing to major labels; I always referred to them as The Big Three. There was Profondo Rosso from New York; Snake Oiler, an L.A. band who were just a rip-off of Profondo Rosso; and The Strip Searchers, another L.A. band that was a metal-punk hybrid who had more or less been a fluke, picked up by MTV and *Rolling Stone* almost as an afterthought in the wake of the success of the other two bands. I'd watch a hockey game - there's one of their tunes playing before the face-off. I'd pick up a magazine at the barber's - there's their faces plastered on the cover. Reagan's trickle-down theory didn't work for the American economy, but by the time he was on his way to full-time dementia it was working wonders in punk rock. All three bands had released albums on Stinkbomb before signing to majors. When they hit it big, so did Stinkbomb and all of its bands. Our back catalog sales skyrocketed as punk rock invaded the mainstream. I was in a middle-class tax bracket. Stinkbomb moved their offices to L.A. and The Hippie finally gave up pot-dealing for running a multimillion dollar company full-time.

We'd moved into a two-flat in Morton Grove a few months after the last tour. Me and Sylvia and the two German Shepherds I'd picked up from the shelter. I got this clever idea that the solitude offered by suburbia would help me. I could start writing more; work harder on my *Punk Bible* column to improve my writing and lose my increasingly desperate attempts to keep the hate mail pouring in, maybe work on a screenplay or a novel. Ease myself out of punk rock and start doing something different; something that I hadn't beaten into the ground. Sylvia quit her job and with a loan from the bank and some money from me, opened a record shop in Downers Grove. She was working between twelve and fourteen hours a day and barely making enough money to cover her share of the rent. I didn't mind; I was making good money and it was a chance for me to help her out the way she'd helped me when I'd first started living off the band. Her Bachelor's degree in art history had become worthless, at least in her mind. She was settling down and trying to start to live a normal life.

****

Our anniversary came up and Sylvia didn't put up much of a fight when I said I just wanted to stay home, order in some food, take it easy. I bought her some lingerie - I never knew what kind of gifts to buy her and lingerie was always a safe bet. She handed me a big box, gift-wrapped. I opened it. Clothes. Really lame clothes. The kind of stuff you see guys at a dance club wearing. Cutting edge fashion. I was too shocked to stop the words from coming out.

"What is *this*?" I was laughing.

"It's clothes!"

"Are you serious?"

"Yeah. You should start dressing nicer."

"What?"

"All you ever wear is t-shirts and jeans, and those boots. You've been wearing those same ugly boots since I met you."

"Hey, I got those boots from a friend in rehab, right, and he's dead now. They have sentimental value. Besides, they're in good shape."

"You've had them since you were seventeen. They're all dirty and beat up. You're still dressing like a teenager. Every day - jeans and a t-shirt."

"Don't ever ask me why I'm an atheist. If there was a god this conversation wouldn't be happening."

"Just try the clothes on."

I picked up the suspect shirt. White. Bland. I couldn't describe it if my life depended on it. Slacks that looked like something you'd wear to a wedding. Another dumb shirt. A sweater.

"Did you save the receipt?"

"Try them on! Please!"

I took off my jeans and put on the slacks. They were about eight sizes too big.

"I can get those fixed."

"I'll get *you* fixed. You're fuckin' crazy, you know that? Trying to dress me up. Where do you get the balls to try to make me your little Ken doll?"

"Asshole! You'll never change! You're always going to be this way, aren't you?"

"Fuckin' bet on it. If change means dressing like one of those douchebags you hang out with in those trendy bars then you've hit the fuckin' nail on the fuckin' head, pussycat."

And then she started crying and she went into the bedroom and slammed the door. And of course, I felt guilty. And then pissed for feeling guilty. I gave her an hour to pout, then I went in.

"I'm sorry," I said. "I just don't like being told I'm a slob and I really don't wanna wear that stuff."

"Can't you just try?"

"Why? I'm happy the way I am. You used to be happy with it too."

"No, I never was."

"Yeah you were. Don't you remember? You used to think I was dangerous. You got a kick out of me."

"Well, you don't have to wear jeans and a band t-shirt and those boots every time you walk outside. Tattoos, that fucking leather jacket, why the hell do you always have to be a punk? You're an adult! Why do you have to keep on dressing like a teenager?"

"I don't have to do anything. But that's what I like and that's what I am. I don't try to dress you, so don't try to dress me."

And then she really broke down, the way she always did, and started apologizing between the tears.

"It's okay," I said. "You can bring the stuff back. Just please, promise me you won't do that anymore. No more playing dress-up with me."

"I won't. I love you."

"Yeah, I know you do. I love you too."

Automatic. No thought, no feeling, just "I love you." And it worked on both of us just like a bad tearjerker works on a lonely housewife.

TWENTY-ONE

With punk rock becoming big business, bands started hiring managers and agents, started wheeling and dealing. Some of 'em signed to major labels, hoping to catch the same wave The Big Three were riding, maybe actually believing that raw talent had anything to do with big-time success. A few were successful; most of them crashed and burned. The punks drew lines in the sand and nearly everybody in a band over the age of twenty-five crossed them, smiling. The ones who didn't decided we were the enemy. I suppose we were. We were all greedy; high on the possibility of being rich and famous. Me, I'd take rich. Famous I could do without. But make no mistake, I wanted the money, and I didn't care what the punks thought. Not anymore. Fuck them, I had bills to pay. I quit writing my column for *Punk Bible* just as the editor started bashing my band, saying we were nothing more than a money making machine; we weren't real punks anymore. That was fine with me.

I'd made it clear to anyone who would listen that I was never again going to tour the punk circuit. Vic was the only one in the band who was in agreement with me - he'd come to hate the fans even more than I did. He hung out by himself in the van before gigs and if a fan approached him and tapped on the window, he'd always say the same thing: "I'm busy. Fuck off." If they gave him shit for being a rock star or a sell-out, they'd either beat it when he stepped out of the van or end up on the ground trying to clean up their own blood. It was getting dangerous to bring him on the road.

Jimmy always took it easy - he never cared about what the fans thought but at the same time he never cared about what was important to me - morally and ethically - as far as the business of the band went. And Simon didn't give a shit about anything besides impressing the fans and being noticed. No big deal. There was a whole new can of worms anyway. Just after we got back from a summer tour to promote our sixth album, Snake Oiler asked us to open for them for two weeks in Japan in the Fall. At the time, Snake Oiler were well on their way to selling fifteen million copies of their major label debut. I don't know why they asked us to open; we'd only met them once when they'd opened for us in Chula Vista in '91 so I could only assume that they wanted to retain some punk rock credibility in the face of mainstream success by having a genuine punk band on their tour. They sucked; in a just world, they would've been lucky to open for us.

Touring Japan was going to be expensive for us. We had to buy plane tickets, rent gear, and a van, and pay Al, a driver and a tour manager. When I suggested that we manage the tour ourselves, Bobby, the office manager at Stinkbomb, pointed out that we needed someone with experience for a tour of this magnitude, at least while we were in Japan. We quickly realized we were going to lose money. I was against the idea. Even moreso when Snake Oiler asked us to accompany them on their two week European tour and their monthlong U.S. tour after the Japan stint. Everybody but me wanted the tour to happen so I promised myself I'd at least try to have some fun with it but the only thing that really appealed to me about the tour was knowing that we'd be alienating a lot of punks.

So we ended up on a doomed tour for two months with Snake Oiler. We knew we'd lose our shirts on the tour, but there was something bigger brewing. I was as stupid as the other guys about it, but at least I smelled something wrong. All they smelled was money. I smelled money too, but I smelled something else underneath it and it was rotten. I wasn't particularly smart or observant, but how could you *not* smell it; the overpowering stench of fresh, quality bullshit? The orange stuff the school janitors poured over some poor kid's pile of vomit smelled just as bad as the puke; it was just there to make you *forget* about the puke. You can't polish a turd? Tell it to L.A. The trick isn't so much to cover up the stench as it is to make you not want to smell it. The Emperor was buck naked but all we saw was his nice three piece suit. And we wanted one too.

I called up The Duke and asked him if he wanted our old van. I knew his band was about to head out on tour and their van had shit the bed. I hadn't talked to him in a couple of years but I was still shocked by his reaction.

"Aren't we benevolent?" he said in his proper English accent. "Mr. Rock Star sells his ass to corporate America and decides to throw a bone to the poor sods who still give a shit about integrity."

"What?"

"You're a fuckin' sell-out, mate, and if you think I'm going to take your charity just because I'm broke and you're a rock star then think again."

"You're talking to me about integrity? You're the one who was bashing that sixteen year old girl in every fanzine in the country because she was complaining after your rabid dog bit off half her face when you left her alone with it while you went out to get beer."

"Spoiled suburban rich cunt, she was."

"Your fuckin' dog almost killed her, you imbecile! And you spent a year raising money to fight the courts so that vicious fleabag wouldn't be gassed by the county. Fuck, three years ago you were begging for change outside the Stock Exchange, you fuckin' hypocrite."

"No, matey, there's only one hypocrite around here and we both know who it is."

"You dumb limey fuck, does it meet your musically correct standards if I give the van to Goodwill?"

"Honestly, I don't care what you do with it, friend. I'm just telling you I'm not riding in a vehicle that reeks of MTV and Pepsi Cola adverts."

"It's *ads* you English dink. *Ads!*"

I hung up and called the junkyard. Fifty bucks. Business as usual.

****

Fifteen million records translates into a lot of bodies. We played sold out arenas every night; ten, eleven thousand people screaming for Snake Oiler. We were just the openers. And I liked it that way. Nobody had the slightest idea who we were; nobody cared. Nobody cared enough to spit, throw bottles, or nine-volt batteries, or their own shoes. Nobody cared enough to scream out song titles like we were Lynyrd Skynyrd. Nobody gave us a second glance when we walked down the streets of Tokyo, buying cans of beers and schoolgirl's panties out of vending machines and stocking up on ultraviolent pornographic comic books that you had to look at backwards. I watched the guys in Snake Oiler get mobbed. Screaming, crying girls throwing their panties on stage; phone numbers written on them in black magic marker. "I want to fuck you" was what they screamed, but they wanted so much more.

It wasn't just The Big Three that had the panties dropping. There were plenty of festivals in Europe; three, four, five day orgies of punk music, sex, drugs and alcohol featuring bands from all over the States, some who'd been around forever and finally started making some money, and a lot more who'd just recently jumped on the bandwagon.

One of the bandwagon bands, Pretty Stench from Seattle, was playing a festival with us in Switzerland. They invited me into their trailer after their set.

"The Pagan Icons were a big influence on us," the drummer said. "You guys are, like, heroes to us."

What a shame; they were an absolutely terrible band. And they sold about five times as many records as we did. And I fucking *hated* people putting a "The" before my band's name. But you play the game.

"Uh, thanks," I said, unable to look any of them in the eye.

In walks a girl - no more than sixteen - accompanied by the band's grossly overweight tour manager.

"Check it out," the singer whispers to me.

"Can I get a t-shirt?" the girl asks in perfect English. She's a Swiss princess. Just hearing her voice breaks my heart. She's so full of hope but she's so goddamn naive and if you have a soul you can feel something ugly coming on like an approaching tidal wave.

"If you give a blowjob to him," says the guitarist, pointing at the tour manager.

She doesn't hesitate. Heads to the bathroom with the pig. Three minutes later, they're out.

"Can I have my t-shirt?" she asks. Maybe hoping to actually blow one of the jerks in the band. The tour manager is looking at her with contempt. Guy couldn't get laid in a whorehouse with fifty dollar bills taped to his enormous belly and he's sneering at this incredible diamond, this misguided beauty, like she's a piece of shit.

"Sorry," says the singer. "We already packed 'em up in the truck." Then he throws me a t-shirt.

"Can you give me a ride home?" she asks. She's ready to cry. "I only live a few miles south of here."

"We're going north" says the pig tour manager. "Sorry."

For once I'm at a loss for words. I thought this was punk rock. I never dreamed I'd see a scene out of a Van Halen home video.

At a loss for words, maybe, but not at a loss for action. I toss the shirt to the girl and walk up to the singer until I'm about an inch away from his face.

"You boys are fuckin' douchebags. Maybe I'll see you again sometime, if I ever happen to swing by a frat party." I turn around and walk out, expecting to get jumped by one of the roadies sitting around sharing a joint, but nobody touches me. Nobody says anything.

When I told Vic about it, he said I should've decked one of 'em.

"Fuck it," I said. "This shit won't last long. They'll be back to flipping burgers in no time."

No, it didn't last long - not at that level - but punk rock had been changed forever and the bandwagon bands would always be around, making money, fucking anybody who got in their way to move another rung up the ladder, and the worst part was, the shittiest bands with the most idiotic members were the ones who did the best. It really broke my heart.

TWENTY-TWO

The A&R stooges; the magazine hacks from *Spin*; even the haircuts from MTV started showing up to the shows, and I made sure we were nowhere to be found. Not out of any sense of loyalty to the punks or what punk meant - and I wasn't even sure what that was anymore - but just because they were scum. I'd learned early in the tour that rock journalists were the lowest form of scum on the planet. Pimps; rapists; child molesters; corpse-fuckers, none of them have anything on rock journalists. They rejoice in misquoting their interview subjects. They take pleasure in making bands look even more stupid than they are, just because they're a bunch of frustrated dinks who don't have the talent or the balls to get up on the stage themselves. They're bitter, small men; bespectacled, geeky phonies who think they're smart just because they happen to be slightly more intelligent than the average idiot musician. Making up bogus facts because they're too goddamned lazy to look for the truth and too goddamned arrogant to listen to it even as it's staring them in the face; convinced that their articles are the definitive insights into somebody else's life's work when all they have is a handful of notes and an ability to tell you what year the third Rolling Stones album was released; waxing poetic about lyrics that mean nothing and knocking tunes that change lives; puking out utter nonsense from their computer keyboards with an authoritative and condescending finality and wondering why music fans hate their guts. The fuckin' fans know more about rock and roll than the journalists do. All the journalists have is a college degree and an incomparable talent for sucking ass, stabbing backs and then moving on their oily way. We weren't hot enough to be of any interest to them, but I didn't even want to be in their presence. Spend ten minutes with a rock critic and you'll find yourself scrambling for a case of Dial and the nearest hot shower.

Not that the A&R people and promoters were any better, but there weren't many of them until we got back home. Japan had been a riot; a twisted version of America if the 1960's had never happened, and Europe had been fun; a new country every day, a tour manager, a driver and a nice van. We didn't have time to think about the business. But by the time we got back to the States I'd gotten paranoid. I didn't trust anybody's smile and every handshake felt slimy. I was the tour manager, and me, Jimmy and Al were the drivers. Vic was too drunk to ever get behind the wheel and even though Simon had given up alcohol and pot he was too goddamned flaky to be piloting nearly two tons of metal, gear, swag and flesh. Our new van was fine, but instead of a TV and VCR built into the van to keep us entertained like we'd had in Europe, we kept ourselves occupied by arguing, fucking with each other or just trying to avoid conversation altogether.

But I still got up on the stage every night; robotic; brain switched off; staring straight ahead. So what? So I had a sense of disgust about the whole thing - not just the tour, but the whole three years that punk was hot. Did I expect a blue ribbon for only playing the game halfway? I was still playing it; what the fuck did my goddamn feelings have to do with it?

When I got really bored, I'd crowd bait, but even that wasn't as much fun anymore. Just something to shake things up a little. Peer into the crowd. Make fun of the band names plastered all over their t-shirts. Tell 'em they're suckers, consumers, fools. Listen with a twisted sense of pride as 10,000 people boo you and you say into the mic, "Get on your knees and blow me, you stupid motherfuckers." Leave the stage with a big grin on your face, both middle fingers extended.

****

Simon loved being in the big time rock world. We'd had his number for years, but he finally stopped trying to hide his desire to be a rock star. The rest of us kept to ourselves, stayed in the backstage area. Each night, Simon went out to the merch stands and stood there, all-access pass in plain view, marker in hand, waiting for people to ask for autographs. He claimed he was just establishing a good rapport with the fans - he was doing it for the *band* - but we knew the score. One night when Snake Oiler's bassist couldn't be found for the soundcheck, the guitarist asked Simon if he would fill in. Simon ran up to the stage and proceeded to run through two Snake Oiler songs. He played them note for note, perfectly. He knew those tunes better than he knew ours. We started joking about Simon taking out Snake Oiler's bassist; a little cyanide in his beer; a shove in front of the tour bus. But it had become obvious that if anything ever *did* happen to the bassist, Simon would've bailed on us in a heartbeat.

****

For the whole tour we'd been taking turns to see who could peel an entire apple in one slice with my Swiss Army knife. Just before our set in San Antonio it was my turn. Halfway through, I cut my thumb open. Al got the hydrogen peroxide from the van and I slapped a couple of band-aids on the cut.

About two minutes into our set, the band-aids fell off and the cut opened up from my thumb brushing up against the guitar strings. My hand was bloody, the strings were all rust-colored and there were little red drops all over my guitar and on the stage in front of me. And as we kept playing, I could feel the cut getting bigger. So I wasn't in the best of moods when I felt myself getting pelted by something small and hard, over and over. Al found the offender in the crowd. It was a kid - maybe seventeen, eighteen tops - who had a pocketful of washers. Al grabbed him by the arm and tried to pull him over the barrier. He wasn't coming willingly. I jumped off the stage and grabbed him around the throat with both hands. That took some of the life out of him. We got him over the barrier and had security toss him. I got back up on stage.

"Any of you other douchebags wanna throw shit at me?"

Pennies, nickels, an occasional quarter. Shoes, class rings, pens, a tape recorder, you name it. I saw it all coming. Didn't get nailed.

"You better stop it or I'm telling all your moms."

"Didn't your mother ever teach you any manners???" Shit, that was *my* line, being screeched by a sixteen year-old girl with a look of chronic constipation on her face.

"No, but my mother taught me calculus after watching the inspiring performance of Edward James Olmos in *Stand And Deliver*." You can *not* let the fuckers one-up you.

A huge, booming, collective "*Fuck you!*"

"Fuck you too, scumbags. This last tune goes out to every sucker who paid twenty bucks to get crammed into this dive to listen to this crap. We're Pagan Icons from Chicago, and don't forget the name 'cause it'll be the one on the license plate of the van that runs you down while you're making your way back to your mommy's Subarus, you little pederasts."

And we kicked into the last tune.

All that crap was just to break up the monotony of a long, boring tour. Like a snort of coke; a brief moment of pure joy followed by the depressing knowledge that it didn't mean anything. Over before you knew it and you weren't any better off. It wasn't a political statement; it wasn't meant to say anything about the world we temporarily inhabited. And the punks knew it. We were still with Stinkbomb Records, but we'd crossed a line and I was perversely pleased about it. Let the crybabies and the dogmatic little pissants - and I used to be one - wet their pants over our transgressions. I wanted to alienate them, not that I had anything in particular against them; I was just dying for reason to give it all up. Drive me out, make me a pariah, fuck my old friends - they could write me off and I'd piss on their graves - give me a reason to be bitter and jaded because simply being publicly, loudly bored with the same old bullshit wasn't making an impression on anybody. Problem was, I had nowhere else to go.

So the crybabies cried and the whiners whined but we still sold plenty of records and we watched as new bands came along and, inspired by us and the other Stinkbomb Records bands, kept the same stupid wheel turning in the same stupid circles, thinking things must've been so great in the "old" days - what, three, four years ago? - never knowing about all the drunken, brutal arguments, the shitty, boring, horrible gigs, the times we'd been screwed and taken it because it was pretty much expected; the sheer pointlessness of it all. You wanna be in my shoes? Take 'em. Have a blast, kids.

By the time I got back from tour, I decided once and for all to give in. Give up. Accept my fate. I was an old fart still whistling the same old tune and I'd keep on doing it until it stopped putting food on the table.

TWENTY-THREE

Even as the heat from the punk rock explosion began to die down, we were still, amazingly, a relatively hot commodity. Sure, your average *Rolling Stone* reader didn't know us from Butch Dickhead and The Fuck You's, but in the underground - which had quickly taken a spot on the outer edge of the mainstream - we were hot shit. Kind of the way a Led Zeppelin cover band must feel when they play to a packed house in some suburban bar. We were getting a ton of local press, tracks in Hollywood movies, even a three page piece in Spin. As far I was concerned, we were a medium-sized fish in a little mud puddle but the checks kept coming in. I couldn't figure out why, but people were paying. And we weren't about to turn the money down. Ever see a bum turn down a quarter just because he doesn't like the look on the guy's face who gave it to him? Right.

Me and Jimmy still got along. Ever since we were kids we'd known we were very different people, but we always stuck together. Vic and I got along okay for short periods of time, but we stayed away from each other when there wasn't a gig or a rehearsal or an album to be recorded; maybe that's the only reason we still got along. Simon was a schemer; he always acted like everything was okay, but he'd bitch and moan about us behind our backs. His girlfriend was showing up at rehearsals and it was obvious she was putting even crazier ideas into his head. He started getting bold. Complaining about what he was getting paid, wanting to get songwriting credits for coming up with brilliant ideas like playing a note up an octave for a few beats, even bitching about where he was placed in promo photos. The only thing me and Vic had in common anymore was our hatred for Simon. But it was a business. You don't always like the people you work with, right? Tough shit. You get along or you beat it. And we all wanted the money, even Jimmy. But at least he had brains and he could keep the peace. Just by being there he calmed things down. Jimmy was always levelheaded. He always had a dry, quiet comment that would ease the tension a little; cause the grip around the beer bottle to loosen so it didn't end up smashed over somebody's head.

We'd been playing music for fun, and when it stopped being fun we kept doing it anyway because we didn't know what else to do. Make a record, hit the road, get fucked, get drunk, make enough to pay the rent until the next record; the next tour. There wasn't any plan. We just kept moving on like The Blob, taking up space and fucking everything up along our way. Only we didn't destroy people. We didn't destroy property. We just fucked up our own sense of reality. We just killed ourselves; sucked the fun out of music, out of drinking, even out of fucking. There was nothing left to do but glide. But what the hell, we might as well get the going rate for it. Maybe even convince ourselves that there was still some important difference between a major and an indie. Yeah, we're still the good guys, still fighting the good fight. Assert it. Loudly. "We didn't sign to a major." Try not to choke on those words. The differences between majors and indies had become so small that even discussing it just amounted to nitpicking. Thank god the fans didn't realize it.

****

Sylvia had been moping around ever since I got back. I hadn't been in any mood to deal with her; I was too busy trying to figure out how to keep the band together without every rehearsal turning into a fistfight. After the Snake Oiler tour I'd gotten a call from some A&R

jerk at Warner Brothers telling us he thought we were great and that he wanted to sign us.

"Okay," I said. "We want a million dollar advance and a one-record deal and the advance is only recoupable from that one record. We want fifteen points plus mechanicals. We keep our publishing, don't make any videos, and we only tour if we feel like it."

"Uh..."

"No negotiations. Anything different from that is a deal-breaker."

"Okay, well... I'll get back to you."

Yeah, right.

I thought it was funny and I figured the guys in the band would, too, but when I told them about it at our next practice, they all got pissed off.

"We could've worked out a good deal," said Simon.

"Fuck that shit," I answered. "I'm not dealing with those assholes. I grew up listening to the garbage they released in the '70s and it still makes me sick to my stomach when I hear a tune by any of those bullshit bands."

"Well, they're different now," said Jimmy.

"Yeah," said Vic. "They know punk rock is hot. Why shouldn't we take advantage of it?"

"Oh, I get it. It's okay if we're the Eagles of the nineties."

"No, man, we're *good*. That's the whole point."

"Listen," said Jimmy. "What the hell is wrong with putting out good music to take the place of the bullshit on the radio and make some money doing it? It won't happen on Stinkbomb."

I was too pissed off to argue. I just said "You guys are idiots" and walked out the door. They still didn't understand that it was all a big scam, that there was no way we could win without turning into a parody of ourselves. If they were willing to choose a long shot at fame and money over self-respect, fuck 'em. I'd dumped every goddamn punk rock rule and every major label rule and I'd made my own rules and selling my ass to Warner Brothers or anybody else just wasn't something I was willing to do. Maybe I was still greedy, but I felt like a martyr and it felt good. Those guys were fucked; I was *right*.

Sylvia had become terminally moody. She was driving me batty with her ups and downs. I finally asked her what was wrong, and of course she said there was nothing wrong in a way that indicated that there obviously *was* something wrong. She just didn't want to talk about it.

She went to bed early one night. I stayed up watching a Sox game. After about an hour I could hear her crying. I got up and knocked on the door. No answer. I opened the door and went inside. The room was dark but I could see a shape under the covers. I sat down on the edge of the bed.

"What's the matter?"

The dam burst. Within seconds, she was bawling hysterically, then hyperventilating.

"Slow down. Take deep breaths. Slow."

She tried but it was hard because she was still crying.

"I just wanna die."

"Well, not literally."

"Yes, literally. I've thought about it so much... it's all I can think about lately."

"You can't kill yourself."

"I hate my life."

"Why?"

"I did everything *right*. I finished high school a year early, I went to college and got a degree. I was so sure I was gonna be somebody, do something. And I'm nobody and I'm getting older and nothing's ever going to get better and I can't stand it. Everybody's doing what they want but me."

"No they're not. Most people hate their jobs. They spend their nights in bars trying to blot out the reality of their shitty lives. They get ulcers and have heart attacks because the stress just keeps building up."

"Or they kill themselves."

"But you're doing okay."

"I'm not making any *money*."

"But you don't need to be making money right now."

"That's not it. I hate doing this. I thought I'd be doing better now but I'm still just trying to keep my head above water with this stupid record shop. And I don't wanna keep doing it but I don't know what else to do."

"What do you *want* to do?"

"*I don't know*! That's the problem!"

"Sylvia, when you started the shop, all you talked about was how good it was gonna be. You never stopped to think about the bad things. No matter what you do there's gonna be a downside to it."

"That's a big help."

"Maybe not, but it's the way things are. Y'know, the grass is always greener."

"I can't talk anymore. I can't even think anymore."

She was exhausted. She'd let it build up until she'd snapped. It was nothing new - except for the suicide stuff. I left the room but I kept the door open a crack. I ended up staying up all night checking on her every hour or two. The next day, I let her sleep in. When she got up, I told her I thought she should see a shrink.

"Yeah, maybe."

"No, really. If you're thinking about killing yourself you gotta see a shrink."

"Okay."

She laid in bed all day like a zombie. By the time I made dinner, she was pretty much back to normal. And the next day, she seemed to have forgotten it all. I brought it up a week later and she just brushed me off.

"I'm fine. I was just under a lot of stress."

"But..."

"I don't wanna talk about it."

"Well, you gotta..."

"*Fuck you!*" From rational to insane in a heartbeat. She packed her bag and bailed out to her mother's and I told her not to let the door hit her in the ass. And three days later I was on the phone with her pleading with her to come back and hating myself for doing it.

TWENTY-FOUR

We played a few gigs in the Midwest to support our latest album, *Destroy All Punks*. We had no plans to hit the road; after the Snake Oiler tour, nobody even wanted to think about it. The Hippie flew out to join us for the shows and to talk to us about doing a new record for Stinkbomb.

I played the shows on autopilot, whipping through a forty minute set without so much as a glance at the other guys in the band. The last show was in Milwaukee at a dumpy little bar. Nobody bothered to advertise so only about two hundred people showed up, all from word of mouth. Near the end of the set I started thinking about some movie I'd seen on TV a few nights before. I couldn't remember the name of it, it was just some dumb '80s rock and roll movie. I mean it was really a piece of crap. I wondered how anybody could invest the time and money in such a worthless film. And suddenly I snapped back into reality. I'd been daydreaming for two and a half songs. But I hadn't missed a beat and it freaked me out. I could feel my heart pounding; palms sweating; tunnel vision, like a bad acid trip. Just a panic attack, but a bad one. I was sure I was going to have to be carted away to the mental hospital in a straitjacket at any second. The crowd wanted an encore. I turned to The Hippie, who was standing at the back of the stage.

"I can't do it," I said. My own voice sounded alien to me.

"Sure you can."

"No, I'm freaking out. I'm having a fuckin' panic attack."

"You'll be okay," he said. He was smiling, and he looked evil to me. No, no, I was just projecting my panic onto him; he wasn't evil. Get control of yourself. Ground yourself, buddy. Try to stay in the moment. Try.

We did the encore and I barely got through it; teeth clenched; white-knuckling it. I practically ran off stage afterwards. It didn't make sense anymore. It was just another job. I looked at the crowd and saw people I didn't understand. The kind of people I'd avoided in high school; the kind of people I'd never wanted anything to do with. They were our fans. They were paying our rent. I couldn't get it right in my head. All I knew was that I was through playing for them.

****

In July of 1996, Stinkbomb Records flew us out to L.A. for a meeting about our new album. We tentatively agreed on a deal that would pay us an advance of $150,000 for the next record with a label option for three more. $150,000 advances? Options? Fifteen page contracts written up by Hollywood entertainment lawyers? It didn't make any sense, but we sat there and listened to the sound of that money, just begging us to come and get it.

I didn't like the idea of being tied up with anybody for three records, and especially with Stinkbomb; that whole place had become dark and cold, like somebody had put a curse on them. The Hippie had less and less to do with the label. That was good and bad. Good because I couldn't stand dealing with him anymore, bad because the guy who was taking over the label didn't really know what he was doing. But when The Hippie *was* around, his paranoia infected the entire office; he was convinced all his popular bands were going to bail to majors and take their back catalogs with them, and he succeeded in spreading the cheer.

Regardless, we wanted the money. Sylvia wanted a house. We'd already started looking around in Morton Grove. Hell, I wanted a house too. It seemed like a good idea; a nice little house with a back yard for growing vegetables. Mowing the lawn and barbecues in the summer with the neighbors, Christmas lights and shoveling the driveway in the winter. Normal. It seemed right. After years of fucking around in a band with no direction, no ability to think about the future coherently, it seemed right. And my cut of a buck-fifty would go a long way towards a down payment on a house.

We flew back to Chicago convinced that we were about to make a record. And then the Hippie started up. He couldn't pay us what he'd offered, he said. We renegotiated. Hired lawyers to talk to their lawyers. And it got dumber and dumber. It was the music business, for real. No more handshakes; no more trusting each other's word. A deal had to be negotiated by industry professionals. The i's dotted, the t's crossed, all the technicalities taken care of. We'd done so many records with Stinkbomb for which we'd never even signed contracts, or signed them years after the albums were released. But this was the new way.

We played the game. It was a stupid game that nobody really wins, but we played it anyway. We'd always done business on our own terms and there hadn't been any problems. Now we were playing by the big boys' rules and we didn't even know what the rules were. Let the professionals handle it. Sit back and write checks for their invaluable services while they play games with our lives. We didn't have any real choice. What were we going to do, release the record on a smaller label? No thanks. Years of experience had taught us that the smaller labels were even worse than the big ones. It was all friendly and low-key until you turned your tapes over. Then all of a sudden your phone calls don't get returned. You get vague answers when you ask how many units were pressed. You never see your master tapes again and you never see your royalties unless you work up the initiative to fly to whatever godforsaken town the label is based in and threaten to beat the living shit out of the owner if he doesn't pay you and give you back your masters. Wait outside the fucker's house with a tire iron. Tell him you're going to break his jaw and then break his wife's nose for good measure. It wasn't for me. I was a lover, not a fighter. Leave the ruining of lives to the lawyers.

TWENTY-FIVE

Me and Jimmy met on our own a lot to discuss the negotiations. Simon didn't have two brain cells to rub together and Vic had never been interested in the business end of the band. Me and Jimmy had always done the work and we always would. So we sat down and tried to figure things out, always coming to the same conclusion; the Hippie seemed to purposely be trying to make our lives miserable. What we couldn't figure out was why.

We went out to get lunch one day at the Subway down the street from my apartment. We went in and he ordered a chicken sandwich.

"You know," I said. "I think I'm gonna give up chicken." I wasn't trying to start a conversation. Just thinking out loud.

"Why?" said Jimmy. "You already gave up red meat. Chicken's not bad for you."

"Fucking salmonella. Thousands of people die every year from salmonella poisoning."

"Well, you can get salmonella from vegetables."

"No. Yeah?"

"Yeah, sure. What do you care anyway? Are you turning into Howard Hughes? Gonna stop cutting your fingernails now, too?"

"No, asshole. But I figure if I'm gonna eat flesh, I might as well stick to eating the flesh of those who have wronged me. Y'know? It's like Muhammad Ali said - 'No Vietcong ever called me nigger.' I'll eat *people*. Like The Hippie."

"Uh, Joe, did a chicken ever call you anything?"

"For chrissakes, all I'm saying is that a chicken never did anything to me."

"Well I'm gonna get a chicken sandwich. I'll see if they have any dead punk rocker flesh in the back for you."

****

The negotiations went on for months. The Hippie's intentions finally became clear. He said it was a shame that we couldn't seem to work out a deal, but he was willing to keep trying. But at the same time, he was trying to talk us into going to a bigger label, and why not? Stinkbomb didn't have the ability to sell hundreds of thousands of copies of a *new* release with their limited staff and distribution, but when the Big Three had broken through to the mainstream, Stinkbomb's back catalog sales had made the Hippie a millionaire. What the hell, why not try to convince us to go to a major too? We'd probably flop, but what did *he* have to lose?

We recorded the album - *Scam Of The Century* - with our own money. We had to do it in bits and pieces, booking studio time whenever we could scrape up a few extra bucks, borrowing from friends, raiding the meager funds in our savings accounts. Simon bitched and moaned through the entire process and didn't come up with a dime. His girlfriend had advised him against it, probably told him it wasn't a wise investment.

We always finished drum tracks first so after the first few sessions, Vic didn't show up again. He had a new girlfriend, a rich college girl who lived in a condo in Lincoln Park, and he had just moved in with her. He didn't seem to give a shit how the album came out; he just punched out after finishing his job and went home.

We were halfway done with the album when it became apparent that things weren't going to work out with Stinkbomb. Ever. We'd agree

146

on a deal with the kids who were running things over at Stinkbomb. Then the Hippie would drag his fat ass back to L.A. from his apartment in Germany and shitcan the whole thing. Over and over and over. He obviously didn't want us, at least not unless it was for cheap and we were tied up for a long-term deal. We got a loan from the bank and released the album ourselves. And after having our lawyers look over our Stinkbomb contracts, we filed a lawsuit against them for breach of contract; they'd never paid us our mechanical royalties. Stinkbomb responded with a countersuit claiming that we'd agreed to do another album with them and by releasing it ourselves, we were in breach of contract.

Scam Of The Century was selling like shit. We didn't have an exclusive distributor and we'd spent all our money on production and manufacturing; we could barely send out promo and we had no money for advertising. On top of all that, the distributors we were working with weren't paying us on time. We'd go weeks at a time where the album would be out of stock because we'd maxed out our credit with the manufacturers and we didn't have the cash to pay them. Every time we'd get money in, we'd pay the manufacturers and start the whole stupid cycle over again.

Sylvia was going nuts. She knew the stress was killing me and she was ready to get on a plane to California, walk into the Stinkbomb offices and start smacking the shit out of whoever was dumb enough to get in her way. I was glad that she was backing me up, but I started wondering why she was so pissed. Because we were getting the screwjob? She'd been losing money on the shop for a year. I'd been supporting her. It was only fair; she'd half-supported me back when I'd been living from paycheck to paycheck. But I wondered how much of her anger at Stinkbomb had to do with their treatment of us and how much of it had to do with her worries about the potential of my cash flow diminishing at a rapid pace. It was a cynical way to think and I hated myself for it but I couldn't see things any other way. If everything had gotten ugly and mean, maybe I had too. And despite my reputation - the shit-disturber, the crank, the guy who was always ready for a verbal fight - I didn't have the stomach for it anymore.

And I barely had the stomach to deal with Simon. Long-standing hostilities developed into out and out hatreds. We kept him on because it was easier. He stayed on because there was always a paycheck, and no matter how small it was it was still better than going back to menial labor.

Things weren't much different with Vic. I finally went over to his place early one afternoon when I knew his girlfriend, Connie, had classes. He answered the door with a bottle of whiskey in his hand.

"Dude, what are you doing drinking that shit?"

"I like it." He was looking me straight in the eye but his face was blank. "You got a problem with what I'm drinking now?"

"No, forget it."

"Am I dressed okay? How's the apartment look? Come on. It's only a matter of time before you start picking away at everything so you might as well start now."

"If you're through being a soap opera queen, can I come in?"

He turned around and walked over to the couch, leaving the door open.

"Got any beer?"

"There's a few in the fridge."

I closed the door and grabbed a Beck's from the fridge.

"Are you here for any reason in particular?" he asked.

I sat down in the chair across from him and opened the beer.

"Can you please just cut it out?"

"Sure, I can cut it out no problem," he said. "Too bad you can't. Just think how much easier everybody's life would be if you would just cut it out anytime they asked you to."

"*Okay*! I'm an asshole. I think we've established that fact. I wanted to talk to you about the fuckin' band."

"Yeah, and probably the lawsuit, too. I'm so fuckin' sick of hearing about it."

"Man, you don't even hear half of it. Me and Jimmy are the ones who have to deal with it while you sit here drunk. I'm sorry if you're bored with it but the lawsuit is kind of important."

"No it's not. It's just another fight you picked. I don't have time for this punk rock shit anymore."

"This punk rock shit puts food on your table."

"Well what do you want? I can't spend the rest of my life backing you up every time you get involved in some stupid argument with somebody."

"Look, I didn't wanna get into the lawsuit anyway. I'm just asking you if you still wanna be in the band."

"Fuck, no. No sane person would wanna be in this band. But I'm almost thirty and this is my job."

"It's my job too, y'know."

"Yeah, I know. It sucks, doesn't it?" He laughed, but it was a bitter, resigned laugh. And I knew exactly how he felt as I laughed along with him.

"Joe, it's not just you. You don't bug me half as much as you probably think you do. I'm just sick of the fans and I hate the business and I'm so fuckin' tired of the punk rock rules. You can't do anything without the punks jumping all over you and... jeez, whatever happened to just living by our Band Rules?"

"We were still playing by punk rules back then," I said. "We just didn't think about it 'cause we were running the game. You can't run the game if you're making money. That's rule number one."

"It's still bullshit."

"I know, but here's the thing. We want you to stay in the band, and if you hate the fans and you hate the punk scene, that's fine. I do, too. But we gotta stick together."

"I don't want anything to do with lawyers."

"You don't have to. I'm just saying we have to be a band again, not just four guys who get together every once in a while to do a job."

"Okay," he said. "I wanna stay in the band and I guess if you want me out you'll kick me out. But y'know, you can't make things the way they used to be."

****

Vic was right. But it seemed now that the old days had never really been that much fun anyway. I'd stayed drunk all the time to avoid the ugliness in my own head. Drank, fucked, played my stupid little songs to stupid little people. Watched as they grew old and sick, and so did I. Watched as they drifted away and a bunch of energetic, hopeful kids took their place; fucking *eager* for an injection of cynicism; dying to put in enough time to remember the good old days, which were never as good as they wanted to believe. Lusting after some credibility, some time and experience under their belts so they could sneer at the new crop of wide-eyed kids that came in every three months. Apprentice bullshit artists.

Things sucked as hard now as they had ten years before. The only real difference was the business. And part of the business was playing the kids. The fun I'd had in the past had been in slaughtering sacred cows. Now there weren't any more sacred cows. Nobody cared about politics anymore. Nobody was shocked anymore; everything had already been done a thousand times. You rarely saw a skinhead at a gig anymore, and the ones you did see were usually well-behaved. The only thing that shocked the punks was a refusal to glad-hand; sign autographs; pal around with the little fuckers. Punk rock had turned into a bastard form of Catholicism in which intentions counted more - much more - than actions. Shitty bands were praised for doing the right thing; playing small, cheap shows, being friendly to the audience. Good bands were berated for playing large clubs, for being stand-offish, for retreating to their dressing rooms instead of mingling. It was like the art world. Just work hard, do what others call art, that's enough, right? Nope, gotta get out there and make the rounds. Make the rich assholes who pay your rent think you give a fuck about them.

The girls didn't dress sexy anymore. Hot punk chicks were out. Frumpy and homely was in; asexuals with bad haircuts looking like extras from an alterna-teen movie. Sexy was sexist; holding hands had more value and meaning than a hot, sweaty fuck in the filthy bathroom of a dingy club in the shittiest part of town. I guess I didn't really care anyway. Those girls had been insane. Well, most of them. It had gotten old quick. I didn't yearn for the past; I'd been an idiot. But somehow, and I didn't know how, it had all seemed just a little bit more real. The old days weren't coming back and I wasn't about to try to resurrect the ghost of Punk Rock Past. Leave the fucking thing in the grave where it belonged. But what was left? A big, fluffy piece of white bread with hundreds of thousands of punks attached to it, gnawing away like so many ants.

****

Me and Jimmy ended up at the Subway once a week. I'd order a veggie sub and Jimmy would order his chicken sandwich and we'd go back to my place and figure out how to try to win our lawsuit and deflate the countersuit. Jimmy thought we should just drop the suit, reasoning that Stinkbomb would probably immediately drop their countersuit. I didn't buy it.

"The Hippie's out of control," I said. "He's determined to take us down and I'm gonna fuck him before he fucks us." I wouldn't listen to Jimmy, even when he made complete sense; when any rational person would've listened. I was pissed off and I was going to do something about it no matter who got hurt, even myself.

We were standing in line at the Subway one afternoon when I noticed a couple of kids sitting at a table. Some high school kid and his girlfriend. She was wearing shorts that showed off a great pair of legs. I should've known better, but I couldn't help staring at those legs. We were talking about Simon, about whether or not we should dump him - just kick him out once and for all - and the kids seemed to be paying attention to the conversation. Or were they just paying attention to my inability to take my eyes away from those sixteen year-old legs? We were hardly famous. It seemed arrogant to assume that they knew who we were. We got our food and headed back to my apartment. I stopped at the liquor store at the corner for a twelve pack. When I got back in the van, I saw the kids sitting in their car, parked a few spots down. I didn't mention it to Jimmy. Small town, just a coincidence.

We got back to the apartment and had just started eating when the buzzer rang. The intercom in my apartment didn't work and I couldn't see the porch from the front window so I always had to walk downstairs to see who it was.

I went down and opened the door. The kids were standing there.

"You're in the Pagan Icons, aren't you? You're Joe Pagan."

"Uh, yeah... I'm about to eat lunch."

The girl spoke.

"Can I have your autograph?"

"Well..."

"How old are you?"

"I'm twenty-eight."

"Wow! You're almost as old as my mom!"

"Listen, I really don't think it's appropriate..."

"Will you sign my shirt?"

"Okay, stop. This is creepy. You followed us here. That's a little weird, don't you think?"

They looked hurt.

"See, I've gotta keep a loaded forty-four in the living room 'cause I'm always getting wackos showing up at the door, y'know? You're not *wackos* are you?"

They started backing away.

"I'm doing an autograph signing at Tower Records tomorrow at two," I yelled. They moved towards their car, not turning their backs on me. "Then I'm giving shooting lessons at Bell's Gun Range in Franklin Park at four. See ya there?"

They got in their car and left. Eyes down, shoulders slumped.

Sorry, kids. Remember the guy who used to go to every punk show in town with a pair of drumsticks? Remember how he'd air-drum while the bands were playing? Remember the girl who wore too much makeup and had a laminated Stretcher Cases sticker hanging from her ear like a grotesque punk rock emerald? Remember when the nazi skinheads attacked Adam Arsenic from Suburbicide on stage and the crowd grabbed 'em and beat 'em down? How about Emil and his jeans that had stuffed animals sewn all over 'em? No? Got anything like that now? Any character, any excitement, anything interesting? I thought not. And I don't have anything left in the tank to try to bring any of that back.

****

UPS showed up with a package one day. It was from The Hippie. I opened it carefully, half-expecting a bomb to go off. Inside was a big box filled with tapes - those self-help, success-at-your-fingertips tapes that creepy guy with the big teeth was always hawking on late-night infomercials. Also enclosed was a bible. And a letter, stinking of patchouli oil.

"*Dear Joe,*" the letter read. "*I know things are rough right now and there are a lot of hard feelings between us and I apologize if I've made things more difficult. But I want you to know that despite everything that's happened lately, I only want the best for everybody. And it may come as a surprise to you, but I've made a lot of changes. Please listen to the tapes I've enclosed. They really turned my life around and I hope they can do the same for you. And you may find some solace in the Bible as well. And please remember, I'm praying for you, and for all of us."*

Stupid fuckin' letter stank up the apartment for three days. I had to open the windows and keep all the fans running to get rid of the stench of patchouli.

****

I didn't fuck around on Sylvia because I'd decided it wasn't the right thing to do, but I also didn't fuck around on her because those days were just *over* and I knew it just as sure as I knew the sun would rise in the morning. There wasn't much else left for me and the band. We hadn't become useless to the fans yet - they still got off on the nostalgia factor - but I knew in my heart we'd become obsolete. Money-grubbing has-been's beating the last piece of dead, leathery flesh off the long-deceased horse. Strangling the golden goose, praying for a few more bucks to come flying out of its ass. Dealing with a lawsuit - like I was some sort of big businessman - involving a pothead wingnut who'd gotten even worse now that he'd been born again. Knowing how completely ridiculous it was but not knowing how to get away from it. And still wanting that money. Vic was still shaving his head but now it was to try to hide the huge bald spot spreading from the top of his skull like a patch of dying grass. Simon had gotten so flabby he practically needed a bra to hold up his girlish tits. Half of Jimmy's hair had turned grey and I had a gut the size of Rockford, Illinois. We were a joke.

I developed a prostate infection. Every time I pissed my dick felt like it was on fire and I couldn't get off without an accompanying shooting pain up my ass. I told people it was from getting fucked in the ass by Stinkbomb. But it wasn't funny. I had a pain in my side that wouldn't go away. I had MRI's and CATscans and nobody could figure out what it was. I knew what it was. When I'd sit and clear my mind and let reality in for a few minutes, the truth was right there in front of me. The ugliness, the greed and paranoia, the game-playing, the head-fucking - all that had fucked me up. Infected me. I was sick.

TWENTY-SIX

Scam Of The Century was a great album. Me and Jimmy agreed that it was the album we had always wanted to make. "The album we've always wanted to make." Even though it was what I felt, saying it out loud made me feel stupid. We sounded like the Beatles or U2. Maybe we'd finally really become self-indulgent, pretentious rock stars. Minus the money and fame.

The album got good reviews but it sold like shit and the fans hated it. They said it was watered down. Heartless. Said we'd sold out. Again. We must've sold out about fifteen times already if you listened to the fans. Hell, I'd poured my heart into that record, and selling out? We'd released it ourselves after turning down an offer from Warner Brothers! I'd thought I was a punk but I started to realize that I couldn't relate to them anymore; maybe I wasn't one of them anymore and maybe I should stop hanging onto the label. I was almost thirty; it was starting to feel stupid to think of myself as a punk. But I didn't know what else I was.

****

The album had been out for two months when Vic mentioned that we hadn't had a record release party. I thought that was a good sign - he was showing some interest in the band. He offered to throw the party at his place in Lincoln Park.

Besides band members and girlfriends, there were only about ten other people there, and most of them were Simon's friends, or for all we knew, people he'd met the day before. It was a depressing occasion in spite of the loud music and laughing and chattering away. It was like we were trying to bring back the spirit of the old days, and the only thing that could make me feel less old and stupid about it was more beer.

More beer meant a bigger mouth. By midnight I'd driven all of Simon's friends away and he left in a snit with his girlfriend. By two a.m., it was just Vic and Connie, me and Sylvia, and Jimmy. Sylvia had stayed away from me for most of the night but now that everyone had left we started arguing.

"Where's my keys?" I asked.

"YOUR WHAT?" yelled Vic. Beer had never seemed to affect him but the whiskey made him just another drunk, either mumbling incoherently or shouting. He'd told everyone at the party at least twice that he loved them. He could barely stand up straight, and he was still swigging from the bottle every few minutes.

"My fuckin' keys," I said to Sylvia. "I gave 'em to you when we got here so we'd both remember who agreed to drive home."

"You never gave me your keys."

"I'll find 'em," said Vic, slurring his words. He dropped to his knees and began crawling around on the floor.

"I gave you my keys and I told you that I was going to get drunk and that you should watch your drinking 'cause you had to drive home, remember?"

"Well, I'm drunk so it's too late anyway," she said, laughing.

Vic crawled over to the couch and handed me a paper clip for inspection.

"You're getting warm," I told him.

"Come *on* pussycat, I said to Sylvia. "We promised to give Jimmy a ride."

"I can wait," said Jimmy.

Sylvia found her purse by the front door and started searching through it for the keys.

"They're not here," she said. Vic was still scavenging on the floor.

"Look harder."

"*You* look!" she yelled, dumping the contents of her purse all over the coffee table. Vic attacked the pile like a junkie looking for a dirty cotton ball.

"HERE THEY ARE!" he yelled, grinning and holding up a set of keys triumphantly.

"Those are Sylvia's," I said.

"THEY WON'T WORK THEN!" Disappointment and confusion swam in his red, watery eyes.

"No. Do you have any coffee?"

"OH YEAH, WE GOT COFFEE! YOU JUST SIT THERE AND I'LL BREW UP SOME JOE, JOE!"

Sylvia thought that was hysterical and I was starting to get pissed, but I was drunk and slightly amused by Vic's behavior so I decided I'd try not to start an argument.

Connie went into the kitchen and put on some coffee, pushing Vic away from the doorway repeatedly as he assured her that he was in fine shape to do the job.

"Is it just me," said Jimmy. "Or do all our parties seem to end up like this?"

"Are you kidding," I said. "This is a good night. You don't see me and Sylvia strangling each other, do you?"

Sylvia sized me up for a few seconds, trying to decide whether or not to start with me.

"Y'know, I probably fucked up and dropped the keys," I said. "Let's just get a cab."

"NO CABS!" yelled Vic. "I'LL DRIVE YOU HOME!"

"I think we'll pass," said Jimmy.

"BUT I WANNA!" he screamed, like a cranky kid in a department store.

Now we were cracking up, and after a minute, Vic started laughing too, although I don't think he knew why he was laughing.

We finally got our jackets and headed down to the street. Vic insisted on accompanying us in order to hail a cab. His apartment was on Diversey and surrounded by hipster bars. We wouldn't have any trouble finding a cab, but Vic was determined to be of service.

We stood on the sidewalk, shivering, while Vic hovered between two parked cars on the street, peering back and forth.

"THERE'S ALWAYS FUCKIN' CABS AROUND HERE THIS TIME OF NIGHT!" he shouted. "FUCKIN' ALWAYS!" He walked out onto the street.

"Hey, be careful," said Jimmy, tightening the belt on his overcoat.

"OH, JIMMY I'M ALWAYS CAREFUL BUT I LOVE YOU ANYWAY 'CAUSE YOU CARE! I REALLY LOVE YOU GUYS! I AIN'T FUCKIN' AROUND!"

Snowbanks on curbs in the city can be dangerous, especially in early February when they're mostly ice. It's worse if it's snowed earlier in the evening because you can't tell how much of the snowbank is snow and how much of it is ice. It couldn't have been more than an inch of snow because when we saw the BMW come peeling out of the alley heading straight for Vic and we ran out to pull him back to the curb, Jimmy and I both took a big spill when we hit the bank. I landed hard on the street and saw dark red, and I just hoped Jimmy would get there in time.

****

There was a wake two days after it happened. I'd been in a daze the whole time. Apparently I'd gone into shock after the accident. Sylvia had run out into the street and the EMT's found me half a block down from the apartment looking for my car keys. I'd fractured my right forearm and broken the wrist.

I hadn't answered the phone, except to talk to Jimmy's folks about the wake and the funeral arrangements. Vic kept calling and leaving messages, crying, but I couldn't talk to him. I wasn't pissed at him, but I couldn't deal with him either.

Vic was waiting for us when we showed up at the wake. He stepped out of the car with Connie.

"It's my fuckin' fault," he said. He slumped down on the ground next to the car and started bawling. "I might as well have run him down myself."

"Vic, it's not your fault. It was a fucking *accident*."

"I'm never drinking whiskey again, man, I swear to god, I'm never gonna touch it again..."

"Just shut the fuck up!"

I asked Connie and Sylvia to stay with him while I went inside. About two hundred people had shown up: family members in dark, worn suits and dresses, friends looking uncomfortable in their respectable clothes bought solely for this occasion, and punks wearing leather jackets and blue jeans - they were the people in bands.

The casket was closed. I didn't even know if the body was inside. Jimmy had been shattered by that fucker.

I couldn't even talk to his folks now that I was seeing them face to face. I just walked up to them and said, "I'm sorry." I started to walk away but his father grabbed me by my good arm.

"You were a good friend to him," he said. "He never said a word against you."

"You were like a brother to him," said his mother.

"I felt the same way about him."

"Joe... The wake, the funeral... We appreciate everything you've done to help."

"It's nothing," I said. I'd taken half the money out of the band fund and gotten the rest from a cash advance on my credit card. Compared to why the money had been needed, it was literally nothing.

"But it means a lot to us," said his father.

I nodded, my head lowered. Sylvia walked in with Vic and Connie.

"He better have a grip," I whispered to Sylvia. "'Cause if he starts babbling and bawling in front of Jimmy's folks I'm gonna take him outside and beat the shit out of him."

"He's okay," she said. "We talked to him and he's not gonna make a scene."

Of course, he broke down in front of the casket, but it could've been worse. Jimmy's folks told him it was okay, that they didn't blame him. After all, the guy in the Beamer had been drunk and he was the one who had killed Jimmy on Diversey Avenue. Vic finally settled down. We stayed until everyone had left and we told Jimmy's folks we'd see them at the funeral.

TWENTY-SEVEN

When Jimmy died, the lawsuits died, the band died, the petty arguments died, everything died. They still existed, but only in a zombie-like state. I guess it was the last straw for me, but when Jimmy kicked it, I stopped caring what punk rock was or what it meant. The meaning of punk - the eternal question: "What is punk?" - had finally been answered for me. It was nothing. It was a meaningless word. What does punk rock mean when you get hit so hard by a drunk driver that your bones are pulverized and you're scraped off the blacktop piece by piece into a body bag? The day he died was the day punk died for me. I'd still play the music, but it would never be the same, and it would never be as good and as vital as it was, not just because Jimmy wasn't around anymore, but because I finally started realizing how ridiculous it all was.

Nothing was very funny to me anymore and I wasn't the only one. There was a jaded, bitter grip on every single one of us. Even Sylvia. We were painting by numbers, not knowing why. I had to take some kind of action, gain some kind of control. People were offering to do benefits for Jimmy's family after he died. I told 'em to forget it. The funeral had already been paid for. Even if it hadn't, I would've found any other way to come up with the money. It was just another punk rock rule: somebody dies, you do a benefit. I didn't want any part of it. It was a punk rule and I was out of the game.

****

Sylvia and I gave up looking for a house. Sylvia closed the record shop, leaving twenty grand in debt, and got a straight job so she could have a steady paycheck. It was a shitty job - executive assistant I think they called it, but she was really just a secretary. Our rent was cheap and there was no indication that we'd ever make any real money so we'd stay in Morton Grove and rot. Her at the office bored and frustrated, me at home, not really knowing what to do with myself. Months passed and I didn't do anything. I'd write a song occasionally, but mostly I sat in the apartment and drank.

It was becoming more obvious every day that we didn't belong together anymore. I wanted to try to make things better, not really make things the way they used to be, but try to figure out where we were both headed and see if we should try to stay together. But Sylvia didn't like talking. It actually enraged her. Sylvia fucked good, and she made good small talk, but anything real pissed her off. For a while I was angry about it. I thought, fuck her - she's changed. She's no fun anymore. And after a while, I finally got what was in front of me all along: she hadn't changed at all. That was the problem. I didn't know where I was going, but I knew I was going somewhere - and I'd always thought she was on the verge of leaving *me* behind. I pretended as best I could that things were gonna be okay with us, but at three a.m. when I couldn't sleep and I was laying there staring at the ceiling, I knew it was over. We'd stay together for a while, but that was just a formality. We were through. I just wished I had the balls to remind myself of that for more than five minutes at a time.

****

Me and Vic finally decided to keep the band together. The first order of business was to deal with Simon. Simon's true colors had been showing for years. He wanted to be a rock star. Interviews on MTV. People coming up to him and shaking his hand. Getting mobbed on the street. He was known as the "nice one" in Pagan Icons by the fans. The fans didn't know what a conniving little creep he was underneath all that sickeningly sweet false humility. He didn't fit in anymore and he had to go. When I called him to tell him he was out, he made it clear that he thought I was a liar and an asshole. I'd put up with his shit for years, and to be fair, he'd put up with mine. Why bother? Why keep going? We couldn't stand each other and if he wasn't completely sick of it yet, I sure was. But he still wanted to be in the band.

"So you think I've been fucking you over for six years."

"I *know* you have."

"For what purpose?"

"I don't know. You tell me. All I know is that you've acted like an asshole to me and I've always gotten paid less."

"Hey, you get paid less because you were the newest member, but you got a raise on every record. And maybe I've been an asshole, but I was always there for you. I helped you out when you couldn't make rent. You cried on my shoulder when your girlfriend was fucking The Duke. I was your fucking *friend*, Simon."

"Joe, I've talked to a lot of people and I know what you've done."

"Like who? The Hippie?"

"It doesn't matter. I know about you trying to kick me out of the band two years ago."

"Trying? Are you serious? If I wanted you out, you would have been gone. What, you're talking about when you told us you couldn't make practice 'cause you had to take care of your sick girlfriend and then we found out that you were really on a pub crawl from the north side to the Loop all day? 'Cause that was *five* years ago and I told you to your face that if you did it again I'd boot you."

"Not then. After the last tour. Calling me stupid and lazy, saying I was a rock star. Looking around for somebody to replace me behind my back. If The Hippie hadn't talked you out of it you would've kicked me out."

"Dude, you *are* stupid if you believe that shit! The Hippie is suing us!"

"And we're suing him!"

"Yeah but we're *right*!"

"So you say."

"Man, you're a fuckin' dope. You know this is what he does. He tries to play band members against each other. He lies to them!"

"You lied to *me*. And you talked a lot of shit behind my back."

"Talked shit? Like you haven't done the same? You're looking out for number one. And that's okay, 'cause I'm starting to do the same. Besides, if you're so convinced of all this bullshit why haven't you quit already?"

"I don't have to be your friend to be in a band with you."

"What, did your girlfriend feed you that line?"

"This doesn't have anything to do with her."

"Of course it does," I said as calmly as I could. "And I'll tell you something else. I can throw a rock out my window and hit three people who can take your place in the band, work harder and have more enthusiasm and do it for half the pay. So I'll tell you what, pal. You're off my tit. I'm sick of making money for you. Go start your own fucking band."

He started mumbling in protest and I cut him off.

"Fuck off," I said. I hung up the phone.

****

Me and Vic went out to a few shows and found an eager kid who was a fan of the band to replace Simon. We weren't going to replace Jimmy; it didn't seem right. I'd be the sole guitarist.

I started working out, seriously. Bought some books and tried to learn how to meditate. Quit smoking, quit drinking coffee and all but gave up beer. I felt better. I was taking care of myself. But nobody noticed and I hated myself for caring. Still stupid, still expecting somebody somewhere to pat me on the back for doing the right thing; still too childish to just pat myself on the back and never mind the rest of the world. What, did I think my life was gonna change overnight because I started taking better care of myself? I was still hanging on to the crazy idea that if I changed, other people would notice. Maybe they'd change too. And I figured if they didn't notice and didn't change, then I probably wasn't much better off than I'd been before. But I stuck to my new routine anyway, just made it a habit. I said I was getting my shit together, but I didn't feel like I was getting anything together.

****

Sylvia came home drunk from the Christmas party at her office, hauling a tree up the stairs.

"Hey, we agreed we wouldn't have a Christmas tree this year," I said.

"I want a tree."

"Well I have to deal with the dogs drinking the water and running around knocking the ornaments off the tree. And then they get broken and I end up stepping on them and cutting my feet."

"I'll clean it up if that happens."

"There's no *if* about it. It *will* happen. It happened the past two years. That's why we agreed not to do it anymore."

"I said I'll clean it up."

"Yeah, after you get home from work and I'm hobbling around with bandages on my lacerated feet."

"Why are you such an asshole?"

"Probably for the same reason you're always breaking your promises. It's just in my nature."

"Normal people don't live like this."

"Normal people bore the living shit out of me."

"You are such a prick..."

"You're drunk."

"Oh yeah, I'm drunk."

"What do you call it? Get three beers in you and suddenly you grow balls the size of Brunswicks. I'm telling you right now you fuckin' lush, get that goddamn tree out of here or I swear to god I'm going to set it on fire."

"*Fine!*"

She grabbed the tree and pulled it out into the hallway. The next morning I had to drag it downstairs to the trash.

When she got home from work she was still pissed off about the tree. She went straight to the bedroom and stuck her nose in a book.

I walked over to the doorway.

"Why are you acting like such a brat?"

"You know," she said, laughing, "you're such a prick and you don't even realize it. Are you even aware that I can't have any friends over because of you? They can't stand you."

"Good. The feeling's mutual. They're a bunch of airheads."

"No, no, no, see, you're just a judgmental asshole. If people don't act the way you want them to, you condemn them. You haven't changed a bit since the last time I left. Talk about breaking promises. There you were, snivelling, telling me you'd try. Doesn't look like you're trying to me."

Snivelling. After everything I'd been through in the past year, to have my own girlfriend say that was too much. Call me an asshole, call me a fuckhead, but don't accuse me of snivelling. I started yelling, surprised at the volume of my own voice.

"You fucking cunt! How dare you accuse me of not changing! All I've *done* ever since that lawsuit was filed is change. What the fuck have you done? You putt away every morning in your little overpriced shitmobile to your miserable little job and you get together at bars with the other losers you work with."

I started pounding the door with my fist, hard but slow, methodical. I was ready, finally, to smash her one in the face if she even looked at me funny.

"I don't give a fuck anymore, Sylvia. You're the one who needs to change. You're the one who needs to figure out why you coast along, blocking everything out and never being able to figure out why you break down every six months and decide you wanna kill yourself. You're the one who needs to figure out why you always run home to mom every time things get rough around here."

"Who the fuck do you think..."

"Shut the fuck up! If you don't like what I have to say then pack your bags - I'll fuckin' help you - and go to your mom's and this time don't come back. I should've let you stay away the last time you left. I haven't changed? Look in the mirror, dummy. You're a fuckin' sitcom. Maybe I *am* an asshole, but don't tell me, after what I've been through, after supporting you for over a year - don't tell me I haven't changed, 'cause you don't have the fuckin' right, okay? So make a decision. Get the fuck out or keep your stupid bullshit to yourself."

She was silent. Wide-eyed.

"You're right," she said. "You *have* changed. I'm sorry." I wasn't sure if she was fucking with me or not until the tears started. I told her it was okay, but I didn't stick around to comfort her. It was the same old shit, another re-run, and I felt like puking. My life was a joke. I wasn't with Sylvia anymore, I was with some straight, uptight jerk, no different from the people I saw driving to work every morning while I sat by the window drinking my tea.

I walked into the kitchen and cracked a beer. If I had to go through that same old routine where she cried and I comforted her and ended up apologizing for standing up for myself I thought I'd finally just lose it and snap her neck. Give it a day. Things would be back to normal. Twisted, perverted, fucked-up, deranged, *normal*.

TWENTY-EIGHT

Bobby called me to let me know he had taken over Stinkbomb. He'd taken over Stinkbomb because The Hippie had been found in his apartment in Hamburg, dead from a heart attack. The neighbors had called the cops after smelling the stench; he'd been dead for two and a half days.

I called Vic to tell him.

"The fuckin' guy bought the farm. No shit. Our problems are over."

"Jeez, that's a little callous isn't it?"

"I don't know. I don't care. He must've weighed two-seventy, minimum, and he smoked about an ounce of weed every day. I think he's lucky he made it as long as he did. And if you want my opinion, I think the world's a better place without him. The fucker had fifty-five years to stop being a scumbag and he chose not to. I don't really give a fuck. All I know is he can't fuck with us anymore."

Vic had never liked The Hippie, not since the first time we'd met him, but he obviously thought I was fucked. I couldn't take back what I'd said but I didn't really want to. Vic just didn't understand that The Hippie hadn't been a person for years, and neither had we; we were in the music business. We weren't people. Why should we have normal human feelings when we weren't normal humans? I'd heard that Simon had moved to Wicker Park and become a junkie. I thought it was funny. He'd joined a new band and they were junkies, so he'd become one too. Anything to keep things moving ahead, keep his shot at superstardom alive, even if it killed him.

We dropped the lawsuit and Bobby immediately dropped the countersuit. Stinkbomb picked up *Scam Of The Century* for a fifty thousand dollar advance and it finally started selling. In fact, it sold like crazy. We renegotiated our old Pagan Icons contracts with Bobby to get a higher royalty rate. Filing the countersuit against us - even though we'd started it and even though they'd ended up dropping it - had made them look bad. Their bigger bands were all jumping ship. Making up with us was good P.R.

The band got together and recorded a new album, *...And The Horse You Rode In On*, for a $200,000 advance. We thought we'd given the fans what they wanted. Twenty loud, fast tunes. The formula; the one we'd been perfecting for thirteen years. The hardcore fans ate it up but it wasn't moving too well. The punk boom had started to die down and we were yesterday's news. The album would never sell enough copies to make back the advance.

We didn't tour. I couldn't bring myself to go back out on the road and deal with the fans. We were exactly what I'd always hated; exactly what I'd always been afraid we would become. We were a Vegas act. And I didn't care what happened to me, there was no way I was going to drag myself up on stage and play a bunch of meaningless songs from thirteen years ago to please the fans. I'd always managed through somehow. And if I ended up laying in a gutter, drunk and splayed in a pool of my own puke, how much worse would it be than playing Jerry Lewis to a gaggle of nostalgia-hungry kids? Really, what was more humiliating?

The past three years had been so disheartening, so vile, so fucking depressing that I wasn't about to add to it by purposely doing things that would make me miserable. I stopped forcing myself to be cold. The Hippie had been a prick but I didn't really want him dead - I'd just been forcing myself to feel that way. I didn't want him alive and making my life more difficult, but I didn't want him dead either. And I'd hated Simon but I didn't want him killing himself with smack. I'd tried not to think about Jimmy while we recorded the album and for the most part I succeeded, but why? He'd been my friend for over twenty-five years. We'd started the band together. And I'd forced him out of my mind during the recording because I was scared that it would feel wrong and I didn't want to deal with anything that wasn't cut and dry. I was tired of questions, and conflicting emotions, and degrees of right and wrong. I wanted everything black and white. But acting that way was just fucking up my head even more.

I didn't want things to keep changing - no, that was the wrong word - I didn't want things to keep *mutating*. I finally started thinking clearly and I started to realize that I had to deal with what was right in front of me first and move on from there. If things were going to get better, it had to start with me. But I'd been infected for a long time and it would take a long time to recover. I knew that and I accepted it. I wasn't sure what to do but I knew I had to start by feeling again, even if it was just a little bit at a time.

I knew something was chronically wrong with me and Sylvia but I refused to think about it. That would be biting off a little more than I could chew. We got along like an old married couple; argued like crazy whenever the conversation turned to something real, but we both made sure that rarely happened. We watched TV. Played cards. Fucked by numbers. Tried not to think about how completely bored we'd gotten with each other.

I'd made enough money from the advance to buy a nice house in the city, in Jefferson Park. We closed in late October of '98. Our monthly payment was double what we'd been paying for rent in Morton Grove, but it was worth it. It was a pretty big place; three bedrooms. I bought a nice stereo system - the first new stereo I'd ever owned - and a king sized bed. And I had a huge office where I could write and work on tunes. Even a guest room, though we hadn't had many guests in years.

The move was hell. Al, our roadie and now my only friend besides Vic, had moved to town that Spring and we'd put him up for a few months until he could find his own place. He returned the favor by helping me with the new house. Moving, painting, making minor repairs, all that. Sylvia wasn't around much because of her job. She'd come home at 5:30, look around the house and make snide comments under her breath. We'd bust ass all day and she always had a problem with the work we'd done. Nothing was good enough for her. I'd paid for the place. Every penny. She hadn't put in a dime. But I was the asshole. Same old story.

Al got sick of it. I couldn't blame him. He wanted to help me out but he was tired of the smart-ass comments about the paint job, the chips in the walls from moving furniture, every goddamn thing Sylvia could find to complain about. She wasn't even bothering to treat Al like a friend; she talked to him like an employee, bossing him around and pointing out all the defects in our work. I told Al to forget it. I'd finish it myself.

I'd spent all my money on the house and the remodeling and repairs. New carpet and furniture, the bed, a dishwasher, lawn mower, new toilets and sinks in the two bathrooms. Dwayne, Sylvia's stepfather, came by a few times to help out. I wasn't a bum anymore; I was legitimate. He and Sylvia's mom knew how much money I'd put into the place. Sylvia's mother - the one who'd hated me since I was seventeen - a stupid *kid* - thought I was okay now. She'd warned Sylvia off me, said I was too much like her father. Well, maybe she still didn't like me, but how could she not respect me? After all, she'd read my name in the newspapers. I was for real. *Rolling Stone* had run a five page article on the band covering our entire history. Of course, back when I really had been genuine - when I'd been doing all the things for which the press was now patting me on the back - I'd been a fucking bum; a drunken, shiftless creep, not good enough for the bitch's daughter. It was only when the band had been accepted by the mainstream that I'd become worthy in her eyes; in the eyes of anybody who only understood nine to five, chasing the phantom American Dream. Well, what else could I expect? All they understood was money. If you were working and making money, you were good. If you weren't working and weren't making money, you were bad. They were like everybody else and why should it come as a surprise to me? TV spoke the truth. Everything was fine. Me and Dwayne got along just fine. Sometimes Sylvia's mom even threw a kind word or two my way.

It was a nice little flip-flop; Sylvia hated me now but her folks thought I was responsible and normal. How could I have gone fourteen years without realizing that I was a stage in her life, one that had been designed to piss off a sixteen year-old girl's mother; a walking middle finger that she should've snapped off after a few months?

The fights got worse. Standing in my soon-to-be office with a roller, Sylvia screaming that I'm going to get paint on the new carpet. Rushing around trying to set up the dropcloths properly. Trying so hard to keep everything pristine that she runs into me and BLAM! a gallon of paint tips over on the carpet. Now she's yelling, and she grabs a roller extension from the floor, holding it at my chest like a bayonet. Angry little German girl, seething, screaming profanities at me. I'm trying not to laugh, holding it in, taking deep breaths in through my nose to keep from busting out like I always do when this four foot ten wildebeest flies into a rage. And I just say "Fuck you" and walk out. Go into the bedroom. Punch the wall so hard I break a finger.

****

I lost twenty pounds. Ran, lifted weights, did push-ups and sit-ups, ate right, tried not to drink as much. I'd slacked off, gotten fat with the move. Now I was back to the old grind. What everybody said made you feel better. I still didn't feel any better but I figured it would take time. I'd abused my body and my mind for over fifteen years - how could I think I'd make it right in six months?

The new place had an evil vibe. I kept waking up in the middle of the night feeling like I didn't belong. Sylvia next to me, snoring, or talking nonsense in her sleep. And me, staring at the ceiling, feeling like crying, but I hadn't cried in fifteen years. I wanted to; I'd just forgotten how.

I was a neurotic. A social spaz unable to be around people unless I made myself the center of attention. Joe Pagan: comes complete with obsessive-compulsive tendencies, and as a bonus, episodes of high anxiety and occasional panic attacks; act now and we'll throw in a batch of insecurities and a year's supply of The Joe Pagan Special Formula brand of bullshit designed to make yourself feel better by knocking others. Popping Valium and Xanax like they were Tic-Tacs and wishing I could find some opium instead. So many years ago, just a kid, trying every drug that came along. Acid, speed, coke, pot, they all just made me paranoid, made my problems worse. An occasional bootleg Quaalude from Mexico if I was lucky, that would calm me down, put me to sleep. But the opium, when I could get my hands on it... that sweet, perfumed smoke filling my lungs... off to the land of dreams... nothing bothered me, nothing fazed me... put a gun to my head and I'd just smile... try to find an opium den in America... the Orientals had the right idea... it's a slow death but at least you enjoy the ride... a quiet world where everything makes sense... where reality stays far away and you always feel right...

It all just got worse. Eat right, exercise, meditate, you'll feel better. Yeah, right. I felt like shit. There was something wrong with this place; something wrong with my life. How different was I from Sylvia? Take away the superficial details and how much better was I than her? I'd been so arrogant, so proud that I wouldn't end up like all the other old has-been punks. I wouldn't end up hitting the same note over and over, endlessly, until I just wanted to drill a hole in my own head to let some of the insanity seep out. And what had I become? Just another sucker.

TWENTY-NINE

I'm not exactly sure when Sylvia turned into her mother, but when I finally started noticing it I could barely stand being in the same room with her. I'd seen the signs for years, but now the metamorphosis seemed to be accelerating at an insane pace, getting worse by the day.

We still fucked, but it was just another bodily function for me, like eating; brushing my teeth; taking a shit. She still came home from work smiling. I'd always loved her smile. She'd always looked so happy to be home, to see me. When she walked in the door, her cruel, German face was transformed into something resembling pleasant, just by looking at me. Now the smile seemed forced and I wanted to slap it off her face. But I smiled back. Ate in front of the TV. Didn't talk. Not real talk. If it got real, it got mean. Sylvia screaming, fists clenched, stomping the floor with her foot like a bratty little child. I tried to keep my voice down. Tried to talk reasonably. And it infuriated her even more. I would've been better off putting her head through the wall; I think she would've respected that more.

There were moments when there was no doubt that she had finally become her mother: impatient with that which was not sensible; frowning on frivolity, save for the type of lifeless, joyless frolicking seen in beer commercials and magazine ads for blue jeans; clinging desperately to a slippery, elusive shadow once known as the American Dream in a heartbreaking attempt to regain some balance and normalcy, some sense of what should be and why; woe to anyone who got in her way as she stormed through each day in a blind fury masked by the most diabolically sweet smile seen since *The Bad Seed*; sinking to desperate measures to make things work out the way they were supposed to; linear, clean, structured, like in the movies - like on TV; trying to force square pegs into round holes and bashing them furiously when they didn't fit; shaping and forming things that couldn't be shaped and formed and raging and despairing when everything fell apart; refusing to back off to assess her place in the world even as that same unpredictable, unstructured world threatened to swallow her whole and spit her back out. She craved small talk over drinks; Tupperware parties with her mother's wide-hipped, Stepford friends. Our house had taken on the characteristics of our relationship; it was a vile, repulsive, hateful little beast and she tired of it quickly. She escaped the blood-red walls of our nicely furnished prison cell for the peace and tranquility of suburban lawns and Weber grills; mom's white walled house; always clean, always safe, always boring but at least there wasn't any confrontation. How terrible it must have been to live every moment in abject fear of conversational depth or self-examination as if those things were like a Mack Truck jackknifing wildly and heading straight towards her; screeching tires that sound like war cries and give off the smell of charred flesh; hot oil on blacktop burning the insides of your nostrils; death screams from grinding gears; fighting against it for her life and not understanding she was killing herself in the process. The world hurt; she would have crawled back into the womb had she been able to. A smile that's meant to make you feel good; head tilted back as she laughs; another beer and unrestrained belly laughs; wet mouth; glassy-eyes; things are good for the moment but there's still a war going on in her head and you don't want to be there, friend, when the alcohol wears off and the depression and anger set in; watch out for flying objects; put a padlock on the medicine cabinet and get ready to call 911 if she goes through with it this time. She was a true master of superficial ho-hummery who had nothing but cold, harsh words for those she called friends once their backs were turned; and when the twenty-ninth crisis of the day reached its peak and she was ready to explode and the frozen smile turned into a grimace, that's when the ugliness began; low, cheap insults hissed through clenched teeth because that was the only ammunition she had; spitting venom at those who dared to aspire to do that which she was too afraid to even tentatively, delicately try. Yes, in those moments it was perfectly clear that she had finally become her mother; all teeth and claws.

****

We'd been in the new house for two months when we had another fight and she stormed out with her overnight bag. The next day she called me from her mother's and said she was leaving me. It would pass like it always did. I wanted it to pass. I didn't have anybody else, and being miserable with someone - even someone you hate - seemed better than being miserable alone.

I got her to come home the next day. I tried to talk to her. She rolled her eyes. Got hysterical. Screamed. And like a dog going after its own puke, I begged her to stay, hating myself for doing it. Scared, too scared to be alone. Maybe there was still a chance we could work it out. I cried, for the first time since I was a kid. But she'd finally made up her mind. Took her clothes and her CD's and her kitchen appliances and the dogs and left. And after the third day; after I'd gone through the hell; bottomed out; wondering who and what I was; after I'd sat and seen and felt things I never wanted to; body shaking; sobbing; after I'd crashed and burned and seen no future, I stood up and decided to take my time. I'd take it slow. Get used to her being gone. Distance myself emotionally, slowly, so that maybe someday I wouldn't hate her. I couldn't stand hating her; she didn't deserve any emotional effort from me.

I did push-ups until my chest felt like it was exploding; ran four, five miles until I could barely stand. Cut into my flesh in order to be the one controlling the pain. No future, but it was still mine.

<u>THIRTY</u>

About a week after she left I was sitting in my room. The guest room. It had become my room. We hadn't slept together in a month. The guest room was the only place in the house that felt comfortable. I slept with the shade up. Let the sun wake me up in the morning. The first thing I saw when I woke up was always the sunlight. The second thing I saw was a print of *The Ship* by Dali. That painting looked like I felt - the half-human, half-boat struggling towards the shore. It comforted me.

I was sitting there drunk, ten in the morning. I'd gone out the night before and bought a carton of Kools and a few twelve packs of Rolling Rock. Sat there getting drunk, smoking, thinking. Thought about calling Sylvia at work, but why? I knew I was drunk and sentimental, thinking too much, thinking the wrong things, lying to myself. Call her for what? To hear more disgust in her silence as she listened to me ramble? To hear that tired, patronizing sigh, that contempt, and hate her a little more? No point. I had to get past it alone.

I got up and walked into the living room and looked around. There was nothing wrong with the house; there was no evil vibe. There was something wrong with me. And Sylvia. I'd always thought I was

179

smarter than her. Sure, she'd gotten a college degree; I had a G.E.D. She'd kick my ass on an IQ test. She had job skills; I was qualified to pump gas and lift boxes onto pallets in warehouses and factories. But I thought I had more insight than her. Thought I knew more about life than her. Maybe I *was* smarter than her but it didn't really matter. That's what punk rock will do to you. Convince you that you're better than the straight people; that you know something they don't know, when all you're doing is flopping around like a dying fish in your own silly, made-up reality. If I was still a punk, I sure didn't feel like one. If I still loved Sylvia, I didn't feel it. I loved myself, as fucked as I was, as low as I was, as sick and damaged as my soul was. I trusted myself. The punk rock scene was a lie. I was through with it. Punk rock had saved my life; punk rock had ruined my life. My relationship with Sylvia had been a clear cut case of two people too accustomed to each other to end a terminally diseased union. I'd been clinging for years but it was finally over. I'd acted like an asshole to her for fourteen years and she'd returned the favor by acting like a cunt to me. Pull the fuckin' curtain and call it quits already, I told myself. Cash in your chips and call it a day and every time you think about what a bitch she is, don't forget to remind yourself of what a prick you are.

****

We recorded a new album. It was harsh and raw and ugly, just the way I felt. I'd learned long ago to sequence an album so that the third track was always your potential hit. There was no question. It was only six chords repeating over and over but I knew it had to be that one. I'd written a tune based on Dali's painting, the one in my room. I couldn't call it anything else but *The Ship*. I sang it in one take and after the album was released it became the only hit we'd ever had. It got heavy airplay on mainstream radio and we made a video for it that seemed to be in constant rotation on MTV. It didn't last long, but we finally got our fifteen minutes and the money that came with it.

My voice had cracked as I sang the words and I didn't care and the producer told me the cracks didn't matter and I thanked him, practically getting down on my knees, because as I'd neared the end of the song, I'd started to feel a warped sense of pride, and some semblance of self-respect; in two minutes and fifty-four seconds, I belted that fucker out and cleansed myself:

My ship's coming in and I'm watching it from within
My brain says move ahead even though the waves are
Crashing in my head
My head and body reeling, hanging on
My heart and mind are screaming for a break
The break; the undertow is dragging me away
My brain has water on my brain; I'm fading fast

My ship's lurching in and I've lost most of the crew
The sky's folding in and I'm sinking slowly as my ship comes in
Attached so awkwardly to arms and legs
I crash and stand and float on frigid waters towards the land
At last; oasis, tears fall, I hold out my hands
Helpless; tears fall, I hold out my hands
Helpless; tears fall; I hold out my hands

****

Sylvia had found an apartment just down the street, but I'd never really see her again. We talked about being friends. Stinkbomb released the new Pagan Icons record. We talked about sticking together, maybe playing some shows. I even tried to make a lame little joke when I called Vic and told him, "Band Rule Number 384 - no more girlfriends." At least he was polite enough to laugh. I let myself get drawn into the lie a little. Tried - I really did try - to convince myself that it could happen. Sylvia and I would be veterans of a fourteen year war; old enemies; old friends. The band would mean something this time around. We'd do things our way; not pander to the fans; not get sucked into the money, the business, the bullshit.

But I didn't really believe all that crap.

ONCE AND ALWAYS

THIRTY-ONE

I dream about a girl every night, been dreaming about the same girl for the three months since Sylvia's been gone. Every night I see her and I almost kiss her, I can almost feel her... And I love her like I've never loved anyone before; a love that's almost tangible; a connection; a perfect synergy; a real love. And I wake up every morning overwhelmed with sadness because I know she's not real. None of it is real. She's just the girl of my dreams.

I eat TV dinners every night. Don't go out; don't spend money, except on cigarettes and beer. Regressed again. Drunk, lungs filled with carcinogens, I sit and try to see through the smoke and all the shit in my head and all I see is black.

I don't have the heart to kill myself, though just to keep myself amused I've thought of the ways. Hanging, that's a dumb one. Thought for a second about buying some rope and tying it around the top of the shower stall. Not long enough. Reminds me of something... back in rehab... fifteen years old... never seen anything like this.... junkies coming in, going through withdrawals on the couch in the living room... give 'em a bucket and let 'em sweat through it... fourteen year old girls selling their snatch on street corners to buy smack, sleeping right next to rich kids whose worst crime was to try to slit their wrists in their parents' bathroom... there was a girl named Lorene, an ugly, freckle-faced redheaded girl... tried to kill herself... no class... no ambition... I'd watched a psycho from New Jersey screaming, running down the hall naked, bleeding from both wrists, forearms slashed upwards like she meant it, but Lorene was an amateur... she ate a can of shoe polish like that's gonna give you more than a trip to the hospital for a date with a stomach pump... she was laying on top of her bunkbed one night and she tied the cord of a hair dryer around the top post and the other end around her neck... she rolled off the bed and hit her feet, waking everybody up... all the other girls laughing... nothing like a botched suicide attempt to lighten things up... horny girls fucking mop handles... deranged boys drinking floor-cleaning solution so they could get a trip to the hospital because once you're off the grounds, you get your smoking privs back... Alligator Girl, skin on her arms so scarred up from cutting that she slams forks into her legs to get the blood flowing... spurting upwards like Buckingham Fountain in the summertime... but you don't feel sick... you only feel some weird kind of respect...

Look at the gun I'd bought in '95. Hold it, like I'm going to do something with it. Take it out to Bell's and shoot it, pulling the trigger over and over while the cops and the other nuts plug away next to me. Think about putting it my mouth - I know the right way - point it at the roof of the mouth and pull the trigger. Don't fuck around. Squeeze it and blow your brain into little pieces. You don't wanna end up a vegetable laying in a hospital bed for the rest of your miserable life. What hell could be worse than that? A red devil with a pitchfork jabbing you in the ass, making you, what, dig holes and fill 'em back in while the eternal flames of hell consume your flesh? Ho ho ho, Santa Claus is coming with a sackful of rattlesnakes too, and the Tooth Fairy is there to give you a root canal like the old nazi in *The Marathon Man* - screaming like a baby for the clove oil. Big fucking deal. Hell is on earth. And I sent myself here. I haven't left the house in days. Order in food. Sit and smoke; drink; listen to John Coltrane, Mozart, talk radio, static. And wait.

THIRTY-TWO

Last night I didn't drink. I worked on songs all day without going out for beer, then found some spaghetti and an old jar of sauce in the pantry, still unopened since before we'd moved. Ate dinner and washed it down with a can of ginger ale the previous owner had left behind in the fridge. Smoked half a cigarette after dinner, then put it out and went and sat in my room. I was still sleeping in there every night, even with Sylvia gone. I unplugged the clock and sat there with my eyes closed, I don't know how long. Long enough, I guess, because when I finally tried to stand up my legs wouldn't work; they'd fallen asleep.

I sat back down for a few minutes with my legs sticking out in front of me. What the hell had I been doing? Drinking myself to sleep every night, thinking about killing myself over a fucking *girl*? I wouldn't have believed it if I hadn't lived it. Christ, I'd been acting like a jackass.

The pins and needles finally left my legs and I stood up. Sitting there, I'd seen everything clearly. I'd thought I could stop hating Sylvia, stop hanging on to her, or maybe try to get her to change, get her back. I'd thought the band was either going to happen or not. Black and white. I hated Sylvia and I hated myself for my part in the misery of our relationship. But that didn't mean I had to hate all women and it didn't mean I couldn't love a woman. And I hated what the punk rock subculture had become and I hated myself for contributing to its decline through dalliances with major label bands and attorneys and lawsuits and my shouted-from-the-rooftops cynicism but that didn't mean I had to hate punk rock and it didn't mean I couldn't love playing music.

I finally saw that I was pretty much the same person I'd always been and I realized it wasn't all that bad. I'd been trying so hard to change that I hadn't noticed any changes. I hadn't noticed them because I'd expected the earth to split open; or a light to shine down from the sky. I'd expected something different. I'd expected to *be* different. I was, but not in any of the ways I'd thought mattered. I was still the same person and I knew I always would be, changing slowly, failing only when I expected success. Hope was an ugly lie. I was through fighting myself. I wanted what was here and now - good or bad.

I went into the bathroom and shaved, taking my time. Let the shower get nice and hot before I stepped in; stayed in there until the water turned cold. Got out and pulled on some sweatpants. Got into bed. *My* bed. The one I hadn't slept in for months. What the fuck had I been doing sleeping on the floor for chrissakes? I turned on the TV. What, had I gotten smarter by not watching it? Took in the third period of a Blackhawks game. And I felt right. I belonged here. Sure, I was alone, but that wouldn't last. Put in a little effort and I'd be charming the pants off the girls in no time. Make another record, make another few bucks. So what if it was stupid? So I wasn't a saint. I wasn't enlightened. Just a fucked-up kid in a thirty-one year old man's body. I decided, just before I fell asleep, that I could live with that. Maybe 1999 would be a good year.

****

I didn't dream about the mystery girl, the one who didn't exist. This dream was different than any dream I'd ever had. It made sense. People's faces didn't change; locations didn't move. It was like watching a movie.

I lived in a house, more like a mansion, really, right here in Jefferson Park. I woke up early in a big bed, much bigger than the king sized bed I'd bought for me and Sylvia, the one I knew I was at the moment asleep and dreaming in.

It was too early to get up but I was wide awake. Sylvia was laying next to me, snoring. She'd sleep until noon if you let her. She was leaving. It was like it had been a few months ago. But I wanted her to leave, and not because I hated her, but because I knew she'd already left. I didn't like the way the dream was going; why re-live the past?

I got up and walked through the bedroom door. The place was enormous. So many rooms. And I realized that I owned a record label and it had grown to become a huge business; we had offices all over the house; even offices for our distributors and sales reps who would come by to work when they needed extra space; that's how big the house was. And my friends - the few I had left - lived there too, but I couldn't find them - just offices everywhere I looked, people typing away on computer keyboards, talking on telephones, sending faxes.

The place was buzzing. So many employees in so many offices, all working for my record label. And I realized I hadn't actually worked for the label in years. Just sat there raking in the profits while other people did the dirty work. I walked into an office and everybody quieted down. The boss was here. No fucking around. They didn't know me and I didn't know them. I wanted to bring out the beer, get 'em all drunk; fuck work for the day, let's have some fun. But I couldn't. I couldn't do anything except sit there and watch, because if I did anything different, the poor fuckers would've been so confused they would've just fallen apart. I'd separated myself from them. I used to be one of them but I'd distanced myself years before, had nothing to do with them; decided new people weren't worth my time. I'd stopped giving people chances a long time ago and it was too late to start again now and they knew it just as well as I did.

I kept myself in the dream. I started walking back towards the bedroom when I noticed a small office off to my left; an office that could only be entered from the outside of the house, separated from the hallway in which I was standing by a pane of glass. There was a girl sitting inside the office in front of a computer. I watched her for a while as she typed; I watched her as she opened the file cabinets, flipped through some papers, pulled a few out and then went back to typing. And then she looked off to the east, off at the sun which was still low enough in the sky to make you feel hopeful; to make you feel like there were endless possibilities ahead.

She wasn't my type; she was a punk girl and I didn't go for them anymore, but I was immediately attracted to her, despite her screwy punk rock haircut, despite the trademark mean little look on her face, despite the zits and the freckles. She sat there, not working, just appreciating the sun. She was suddenly beautiful. I knocked on the glass and she looked over.

"Are you from the distributor?" I asked.

She shook her head.

"Are you a store rep?"

She shook her head again.

"I work for Elliot," she said. She told me her name but I couldn't grasp it, couldn't remember it. And Elliot, who was Elliot? A vague memory. I couldn't quite remember but I thought I might know...

"He's a lawyer. He used to work for your band, but that was years ago."

"Oh yeah." I was pretty sure I remembered now but I still couldn't quite place the name. It didn't matter. I always had something to say, even when I didn't know what I was talking about.

"It must be hell," I said, looking into her beautiful, fucked up face, a face filled with hope and love and purity, like the sunshine coming in through the window. She was smiling at me, fucking *radiant*, as perfect and true as you only find in dreams.

"It must be hell," I said again, "working for such a dirty, cocksucking scumbag like Elliot. Why don't you come work for me?"

The smile disappeared. Her face flashed disappointment, then disgust, then anger. She turned away.

"What's your name again?" I asked. "I forgot."

She turned back to me, teeth bared, eyes blazing.

"Fuck you!" she screamed.

She headed for the door. I had a head start; she had to go all the way around the house to get to me; I was already inside. I made for the bedroom. Ran past Sylvia - still sleeping of course - and into the bathroom. I kept the door open and crouched down by the toilet, hiding. I could hear her voice filling the house, howling. If she got her hands on me, I knew she'd kill me; eat me alive. But I was pretty sure I was safe. I was pretty sure she'd calm down by the time she found me, and

I knew she'd find me. Maybe I really wasn't safe, but I wasn't worried. In fact, I had to bite the insides of my cheeks to stop myself from laughing out loud. Oh, she was all worked up! Fucking hilarious! Say one thing wrong and they flip out! I felt great. I felt alive.

"I heard you were a piece of shit!" she screamed from somewhere in the house. "Everybody said you were a dirty, rotten prick! But I didn't believe it! I never knew how much of a motherfucker you were until you opened your *big fucking mouth*!"

I stayed where I was, not moving, not breathing. She was getting closer now and there I was hunched down next to the toilet like a kid playing hide and seek, trying not to laugh my ass off.

She was in the bedroom now. I could hear her stomping through the room, smashing anything that was in her way, coming for me, and I couldn't help it, it was fucking *funny*. I knew I'd wake up before she got to me. And just before I came out of the dream and woke up in my bed with the sun shining through the window, just before she got to me and tore me apart, fucked me up good, I heard her scream one word and I couldn't hold it in anymore. I started laughing an uncontrollable, joyous belly laugh, not caring how loud it was; not caring that it was giving me away. She screamed that word, that beautiful word, as loud as she could, nearly shattering my eardrums; one word like an air raid siren; hatred, violence, bloody fucking murder in her voice:

"*ASSHOLE!*"

I woke up smiling.

Born in Evanston, Illinois in 1968, Ben Foster is a notorious figure in the underground music scene. Through his work as the lyricist and singer in the band Screeching Weasel, his columns in countless punk fanzines, and his rants in self-published zines, including *Panic Button* and *Blood On The Ice*, he has provoked, delighted, alienated and entertained thousands of people. He lives in Oak Park, Illinois with his four cats.